PRAISE FOR *ALL MY FALLEN ANGELAS*

"These beautifully told stories of the lives and loves of immigrant girls and women will charm you and chill you and break your heart. Above all they will hold you, from the first page to the last."
—**Nino Ricci,** author of the award-winning novel *The Origin of Species* and of the *Lives of the Saints* trilogy

"*All My Fallen Angelas* is symphony of female voices of all ages, weaving an intricate web of stories around Canadian girls and women of Italian origin living in Toronto. The narrative I, belonging to different characters, explores a memory, a moment of revelation, a traumatic event. Gianna Patriarca's short stories are threads of a larger texture, probing, with subtlety and irony, the nuances and the intricacies of the mind of women who bear in their very names their family history."
—**Oriana Palusci,** University of Naples, Orientale

"In her new book, *All My Fallen Angelas,* Gianna Patriarca offers stories elaborating authentic portraits of characters in Toronto's Italian community. She dips into her memories of growing up in Toronto to offer living photographs seen through the lens of deep compassion. The experiences of ordinary immigrant Italian characters, whose lives are largely underrepresented in Canadian literature, come alive and are told with attentive humour and grace. Patriarca's stories reclaim the drama of lives, voices, and events from the anonymity of history. *All My Fallen Angelas* is a timely collection of stories of a community known largely through stereotypes."
—**Isabella Colalillo Katz,** author of *Marlene Dietrich's Eyes*

"Gianna Patriarca infuses her prose with masterful strokes of poetic prowess. Her short stories are amazing, powerful, often cool and so very important. She gives voice to the silent and overlooked narrative of the women in our community who have sacrificed and lived so much for their families and also for themselves. The book, however, goes far beyond the stereotypical nonna-in-a-black-dress archetype and finally brings life to the rich, colourful, and complex lives of women who have been overshadowed by stories of romanticized male-dominated mafia melodrama and mayhem."
—**Domenico Capilongo,** author of *Subtitles and Other Stories*

"Gianna Patriarca's latest book of stories captures the tension and liability of being an Italian/immigrant woman. Through well-crafted and engaging stories, she weaves passion and melancholy into the lives of women caught in that liminal space between the old world values and the new Anglo mores, metaphorically captured as the characters gaze out their neighbourhood windows. Patriarca transports us into a world of women with desires and needs which they have learned to suppress out of cultural deference. I highly recommend this book for its gorgeous contribution to understanding Italian women's experiences and for the Italian female sensibility with which it dances."
—**Theresa Carilli,** Purdue University

"Gianna Patriarca introduces her characters with a sharp-eyed gentleness and compassion rooted in fond familiarity. These are stories in which the author is sometimes observer, sometimes participant. They do not end at the final page, but carry on in our imagination, in our emotions. In each of her observant tales, there is something of herself and of myself and of all of us."
—**Linda Stitt,** poet

ALL MY FALLEN ANGELAS

We gratefully acknowledge the support of the Canada Council for the Arts and the Ontario Arts Council for our publishing program. We also acknowledge the financial support of the Government of Canada through the Canada Book Fund.

Front cover artwork: Mimmo Baronello, "Sicilian Raven," 2013, oil on canvas, 36 x 47 inches. www.mimmobaronello.com

Cover design: Val Fullard

All My Fallen Angelas is a work of fiction. All the characters and situations portrayed in this book are fictitious and any resemblance to persons living or dead is purely coincidental.

Note from the publisher: Care has been taken to trace the ownership of copyright material used in this book. The author and the publisher welcome any information enabling them to rectify any references or credits in subsequent editions.

Library and Archives Canada Cataloguing in Publication

Patriarca, Gianna, author
All my fallen angelas / short fiction by Gianna Patriarca.

(Inanna poetry and fiction series)
Issued in print and electronic formats.
ISBN 978-1-77133-277-4 (paperback).-- ISBN 978-1-77133-278-1 (epub).--
ISBN 978-1-77133-280-4 (pdf)

I. Title. II. Series: Inanna poetry and fiction series

PS8581.A6665A55 2016 C813'.54 C2016-900300-0
C2016-900301-9

Printed and bound in Canada

Inanna Publications and Education Inc.
210 Founders College, York University
4700 Keele Street, Toronto, Ontario M3J 1P3 Canada
Telephone: (416) 736-5356 Fax (416) 736-5765
Email: inanna.publications@inanna.ca Website: www.inanna.ca

MIX
Paper from
responsible sources
FSC® C004071

ALL MY FALLEN ANGELAS

SHORT FICTION

Gianna Patriarca

INANNA PUBLICATIONS AND EDUCATION INC.
TORONTO, CANADA

ALSO BY GIANNA PATRIARCA

POETRY

Italian Women and Other Tragedies
Daughters for Sale
Ciao Baby
The Invisible Woman
What My Arms Can Carry
My Etruscan Face
Too Much Love

CHILDREN'S FICTION

Nonna and the Girls Next Door

To my great niece
Margaret Gertrude Catherine,
I leave you the stories because one day you may be curious,
zia loves you.

To my friend, Corrado Paina,
poet, artist, thinker,
thank you for the fabulous ride.

CONTENTS

...[T]o inhale the history of women's lives,
to understand at last this gift.
—Maria Terrone, "The Tatted Handkerchief"

I miei non sono sogni
ma sono spiegazioni....
—Patrizia Cavalli, "Ma questo non é sonno"

My realism is an act of love.
—Pier Paolo Pasolini, in "Becoming Neorealism"

ALL MY FALLEN ANGELAS

...[P]oi che anch'io sono caduta
Signore
e sto qui infitta
sulla mia strada
come sulla croce.

—Antonia Pozzi, "Così Sia"

...[A]nd then I also fell
Lord
and I am here again
on my road
like on the cross.

—translation, G. Patriarca

IT WAS FOUR MONTHS AFTER THE DAY I disappeared when they broke through the drywall. Six by eight and newly painted a basic cream. I should tell you they did not find the beautiful woman I had been. What was left of me wrapped in the cheap plastic from the local hardware store would not tell you anything about who I was, who I had been or what I looked like. I will tell you all this now, because now I can speak without fear and without shame. Nothing can hurt me now. If I had spoken before I might have avoided the plastic and the drywall. I might have avoided all of the harm that came with it. But what we should do when we are able is typically the one thing we never do.

How did I end up behind the wall? How do we end up anywhere? Circumstance? Choice? The wrong exit down the right road? Door number one, or two, or three? I really don't know. The one thing I am sure of is that I would not have chosen this ending. No one would have chosen an ending like this.

The truth is I loved life. Loved it completely like an ice cream in July. But too much love can be dangerous. Too much love can disguise the enemy, obscure the stop signs. Too much love can distract you from heading in the right direction. But as a writer once wrote, "I was a fool for love." Somehow it landed me here.

You ask the inevitable question, "If you could change it all?" Yes, if I could change it all I would go back and do it quite differently. I would make adjustments, alter the outcome. I might even think it through with my head instead of my heart. One thing is for sure, I would go back and I would talk. They would hear my version, my side of the story, my reasons. It would make it easier to finally rest, to clean out that space behind the drywall.

There have been so many stories circulating about me. So many assumptions and imagined shameful allegations about the kind of woman I was, hurtful to those who loved me. Endless fantasies of lurid adventures invented by those who never experience them but are titillated by imagining those of others. People take such pleasure dissecting the lives of others, searching for imagined indignities, revelling in the dirty bits, the possible scandals. It takes no effort at all for vicious mouths to assassinate you without ever knowing the truth. My ending was more material than anyone could have dreamed of. Yes, my life had been complicated, even shocking to some, but it was mine and I take full responsibility for how it turned out. I will not blame anyone else. The mistakes I made were mine as well as the triumphs. I do not apologize.

I was alone behind the drywall. Left in a bundle of plastic bound in duct tape. My purse and shoes tossed in for company. But now I am in a different space, where there are no walls. Here, where I am now, there is nothing to damage or to annihilate, simply a vast space of warmth where we gather without fear. Here we are many women. All of us have arrived at different times, in distinct ways and for an assortment of reasons. We are different shapes and sizes. We are old, young, some barely women at all, still children with smooth skin and bright eyes. Our age really doesn't matter, it is of no importance here. We no longer have a relationship with time. Time is of no concern. Here we can be the women we were meant to be from the beginning, untainted, whole, beautiful and free.

I arrived when summer is most radiant. In those ripened days of June, when the hours are the brightest and the longest and submerged in scents. The seasons of women are endless and each woman brings an inimitable fragrance. My young friend Yasmin arrived with the brisk coolness of autumn. Her teenage body hurled in a burrow by the side of a road, buried beneath a mound of dry but brilliant leaves. They found her whole and beautiful still, huddled inside the earth, near an open field, on a chilled night in October just before the squatter frost returned. They wrapped her in white linen. The hint of sweet oils and incense followed her here, along with some tears that quickly dried on the clearest day. Here, where we are now, the days are eternally clear and tears have a short stopover.

My parents keep their tears as a weapon. Tears are their only defence against the anger they cannot release. They are trapped in all the confusion and unanswered questions. My children have no more tears, only the torment of nightmares. This is my most painful wound. My husband has attempted to forgive my sins and continues to sleep alone in the same bed we once shared. But he had learned to sleep alone long before they found me. He copes. I have left him all the disorder. I have left him all the emptiness. He's a good man who will never be happy. Whatever happiness is, it is never a man alone in the bed of a woman he has loved.

I have left them all this unrest although it was never my intention. Sometimes when we are on the way to the merry-go-round we trip while running toward the prettiest painted horse, and every now and then we knock over the innocent.

I was beautiful. Born beautiful. I had heard the word describe me from the time I could understand language. My father called me "*bella*" more often than my mother did. Mother was less impressed by beautiful things, much more practical about things than my father. She let the word slip only on occasion, fearing I might become possessed by my own enchantment. My grandmother, who had given birth to my father, was less fearful of my obsessions and often took credit for everything that was pleasant in my personality and in my looks. My blue eyes resembled hers, my curls, my pink and creamy skin, the delicate slope of my nose and the round firmness of my body came from her genes. She assured me often that I came from a handsome and clever tribe and she repeatedly, and audibly, thanked her ancestors for the blessings they had bestowed on her children. She claimed we were from a noble line. My ancestors had once thrived by the feet of the white peaked mountains by the River Adige. My grandmother was relentless in reminding me of my great fortune in having inherited the beauty and the light of her mountains. I was sanctioned by the mystical gods of her memory who had followed us to the Caledon Hills where less imposing white peaks were visible only in the icy months of a Canadian winter.

By the time they found me behind the drywall my grandmother had been long gone. I was glad she never knew about the wall. I was glad she had been spared the shame and the collapse of her beloved tribe, her noble family.

I had grown to be tall and slender with cinnamon curls bountiful around my face. My lips needed little colour, they were full and fell easily into a smile. My eyes had the grey tinge of sky after a sudden storm. I charmed people effortlessly. Charm is a wonderful attribute and I possessed enough to make my father proud. I was my father's first child. My father had chosen my name, Alba. He told me over and over again that Alba meant dawn, the beginning, the first light. Alba was a name I never liked. It felt wrong; it didn't suit me. When I was old enough to choose I demanded to be called by my second name, Angela. But my father never once called me by my second name.

At the beginning it all seems possible. At the beginning of everything there is hope, promise, and the pleasure they bring. Little girls who are the beginning of everything live in magical spaces. But we are little girls for such a short time; the excitement of grown up things arrives quickly. When you are beautiful, you cannot live in that enchanted space forever because the world will want to take it from you. If you are not beautiful, the magical space exists only inside your head. You try to make sense of the rules, the definitions, to decode the muffled messages, but it doesn't always make sense, and that is just the way it is. I was beautiful and easily lured into the candy shops. Tempted by the sweetness, the bright colours, by the pink lady in the music box. Little girls who are beautiful are programmed to want everything, and I walked in with the sweetest tooth, aching in delight.

It is pleasant here, without candy shops, without feeling hungry, without the ache of a sweet tooth. It is peaceful here. Yes, that's the word — peaceful — a word we take for granted. In this place nothing explodes or bleeds, there are no earthquakes or heartaches or even headaches. But there is still much to unravel before we find the absolute calm. Some of us, still interns, arrive here carting our wounds on the outside, visible but irrelevant. The wounds no longer define who we are, they are simply a reminder of the reasons that brought us here, together.

Alicia arrived just before Christmas, without the ribbons or bows. The knife wounds were still fresh, all twelve of them. It was the third deep slash that secured her place here among us. The third cut was just below the heart, that vulnerable spot that is always defenceless. It is difficult to protect such a large target. A woman's heart is always a bull's eye. Alicia isn't speaking yet but her time will come.

My friend Yasmin's wound is less visible beneath the long silk scarf that loops around her neck. She tells me how much she hated that scarf when she was forced to hide behind it, and now it is a soft and warm comfort on her lovely skin. We wear things differently here, without meaning or need, without force or obligation. My red shoes with the high heels still make my legs look longer, but now they do not hurt my feet. I wear them but I do not need them. Mother never liked my red shoes. I hid them and wore them when she wasn't looking, without her blessing. The red shoes were there, with me behind the wall, when they found me. The red shoes were barely scuffed.

The day Hanna arrived there was a perfect sunset, the kind that detonates an immense blazing colour in the sky and you cannot imagine darkness ever again. She arrived with her belly still swollen where her son had been for almost seven months. She had not planned this arrival. She had only ever imagined and prepared for the moment she would hold her newborn. That was all she lived for. But that evening it all went wrong when the meal wasn't ready and the house wasn't clean and she was too tired to lift her body from the softness of her bed. And the end came with the usual brutal anger that erupted when she could not meet all the needs and all the demands expected of her. Here she can rest.

Each evening around the circle there is a new face. Alicia's long lashed brown eyes and freckled skin, her bashful and pretty smile were welcomed here today. She's very young. Many here are very young: uncomplicated, innocent. When I look at her I think of my own daughter, my own young daughter, whom I am sure will never come here. I know she will not be captivated by the memory of my weaknesses. My daughter will not misjudge things as I did. She will not be charmed by the taste of what is sweet. I'm ashamed to have left her a sadness she will never comprehend. My daughter is intimate with grief; it has become her confidante. Grief has taken my place, replaced me in her life, and I am to blame. But sorrow will not betray her as I did.

I sit close to Alicia. I take delight in her lovely face, her sweetness. I become a mother again in her presence. We need each other here. Together we will find the calm.

*

I did love him. I really did love him. I shouldn't have, but I did even if everything about that love was wrong. I should have known that. But how does one understand those loves? The wrong ones? They hold you hostage and you cannot walk away. The loves that excite you and make the hours seem short-lived seconds. Those loves that when they walk out of a room, you cannot bare the vacancy they leave behind even for a few minutes. I loved the air around him. I loved the spaces he touched and the floors he walked on. I loved the strength in his hands.

There were moments when the rest of the world had no place in our story. The past, the present, the husband, the wife, the children, were all on the fringe. They were loved but not central. The all-consuming need to be somebody's Venus was too compelling. I should have remembered who I was, where I came from. I should have considered all that I had to lose. But, then, who I was did not matter. Then, where I came from did not matter. What I had to lose I was willing to gamble. I had already jumped deep into the well.

We are not all here because of love. Some of us are here because there was no love. Julia can tell you that. In that cold bed she slept in there was compulsion and obligation, but no love. She brought the pillow with her, holds it close. The pillow set her free. There was no resistance, she didn't struggle at all, let her breath go into the white cotton and closed her eyes. At the time it seemed the better choice.

I fought with everything I had. I fought until that last blow and then the bottom of the stairs. It wasn't the stairs that ended me. It was the strike to the back of my head as I walked away. Walking away, taking charge, making a decision I had wanted to make for the longest time. Isn't it curious how things turn out? When you finally decide you are doing the right thing, life steps in and opts for a different ending.

I have time now to look at all the pages of the diary, the photo album. On my wedding day, my husband and I wore white, my grandmother's request. Mamma and Papa were delighted, had helped in choosing not only the groom, but our garments, our venue, our menu. They were enjoying the events of the day, the attention, both elegant in their outfits. My mother wore her velvet hat like a diamond tiara and my father was given a white silk scarf to slip into the jacket pocket of his black tuxedo. The Caledon hills were green in the month of June as I climbed into the carriage adorned with satin bows. I believed I could make it happen. I believed that it would all come true. It would all turn out the way it was meant to be. I could live the enchantment. I would be wife to the husband prince, daughter to the King and Queen, and mother to the noble heirs to come. I would remain the dawn of every possibility. But it was not long before my husband prince retreated into his private fortress where I could not enter, did not care to enter. Not long before I tired of fables, threw out the music box, and ventured out into the dark, dark woods in search of a real adventure.

A GIRL NAMED ASCENZA

Will we ever live so intensely again?
Will love come to us again and be
so formidable?

—Eavan Boland, "Love"

THE MONTANESI BROTHERS HAD the reputation of being the biggest morons Western Technical and Commercial High School had ever produced. Although, it wasn't all Western Tech's doing. Nick, Peter, and Adamo were Western Tech's rat pack. They were the wop boys you loved to hate but couldn't. They were cocky and arrogant and never missed an opportunity to behave like complete asses. The brothers made each school day just a little unusual and that made school a little more bearable. If they weren't making trouble then they were looking for it and, at sixteen, trouble is cool.

As obnoxious as they appeared to be there was one thing no one could deny about the Montanesi brothers. They were absolutely, incredibly, undeniably, fucking gorgeous. I'm talking Paul Newman and Steve McQueen kind of gorgeous, bad boys kind of gorgeous, with the contagious moodiness of James Dean. I had lived on the same street as the Montanesi brothers from the time I was ten and, the moment I set eyes on them, my heart and my head never quite got it together again.

September 1969, grade nine. My homeroom teacher had on a purple bow tie the day I walked into his class, a purple bow tie with a lime green shirt and beige corduroy pants. I didn't mind the corduroys but I knew from that bow tie that he was not going to be the teacher who would inspire any remarkable events in my life or arouse my imagination beyond wondering how he had come to choose his tie that morning. It was my first day of high school and my eagerness for the new experience had forced me out the door and early to class.

Mr. Yaborski, the purple bow-tie teacher, waved me over to his desk as I entered the classroom. He held out his hand waiting for my admission slip, and as I handed it to him, he pointed to a row of seats and made a motion for me to sit down. But I stood by his desk and waited for his eyes to lift from the paper I had handed him, watching him scan the form a couple of times before he finally looked up at me.

"I can't read the name written here, what is your name?" he asked.

"My name is Ascenza," I said. "Ascenza Letizia Faragalli."

"I'm sorry I don't know how to pronounce all that. Do you go by any other name?"

"Agnes." I said.

"Not much better is it?"

"Not much." I agreed.

The tall windows of the second floor classroom were open to the street sounds that floated on the first drafts of a September breeze. I chose a seat by the first window where I could look out at the trees that lined Evelyn Crescent and where I could watch the occasional bird land and linger a while on the cement ledge. The birds, free, bopping about without concern, then rising to the sky. I sat there with an eye full of Mr. Bow-Tie having stupidly been the first to arrive, waiting for the other students.

I wondered what Mr. Yaborski's mother might have found charming about the name Stanley when she decided to give it to her son. Mr. Stanley Yaborski, my homeroom teacher, taught business, math and geography. I looked at my brand new timetable neatly inserted into my three-ring binder. Thank God, I only had two classes with Mr. Stanley Bow-Tie: geography and homeroom. I could survive that.

The bell rang exactly at nine. Mr. Bow-Tie shut the classroom door after the last student had taken a seat. As he adjusted his purple tie and began his opening remarks, the door flung open and like a fist to the jaw in came Adamo Montanesi, tall, lanky and slightly out of breath. I recognized him instantly. He and his brothers were by now a legend in the school.

Adamo stood at the door bouncing on both feet, shaking his head as if he were clearing something from his ear canal, his untamed brown curls falling over his forehead. "Those bells are way too loud, Mr. Y. Can't you do nothing about that? Hey we're not going to church, right?"

"Ah, Mr. Montanesi. I see I have the great pleasure of your charming company for another year. Oh my! Lucky, lucky, me."

"Pleasure is right, Mr. Y., you know me, I'm all about pleasure."

Adamo strutted to the unoccupied seat by the front window as Mr. Bow-Tie reluctantly lumbered over to shut the door.

As Adamo slid into his seat another amusing proclamation wafted from his lips. "That's a terrific shirt you got on there, Mr. Y. looking good! Where can I get a shirt like that?"

The class couldn't keep the giggling from graduating into raucous laughter, which amused Adamo and fuelled his courage.

"And that tie, Mr. Y., youse got really great taste."

"That will do, settle down everyone. And you, Mr. Montanesi, keep it parked in that seat, and if you are a very good boy I'll take you shopping one of these days."

"Yes sir, Mr. Y., I aim to pleeeeeease."

You had to give Mr. Bow-Tie credit. He genuinely didn't seem to mind the shenanigans that came with Adamo Montanesi and their mutual teasing had a certain entertaining aspect that the rest of us appreciated. Mr. Bow-Tie picked up a chalk, walked to the black board and began printing in large letters: CLASSROOM RULES TO BE RESPECTED.

The year I entered high school the Montanesi brothers were already a part of Western Tech's history. They strutted down the halls, beautiful, wild young bulls who didn't give a damn who or what got in their way. As it happened, nobody ever got in their way. Everyone kept a safe distance and gave the boys plenty of room to swagger down corridors or clamber up the stairs, which they did with complete confidence. There wasn't a rule in school they hadn't bent or broken, and there were plenty of rules to bend and break. They cussed, smoked, and drank beer they snuck into their lockers. They flashed their pearly whites with satisfaction whenever they had caused some kind of disruption and never feared the consequences. They skipped classes and talked back to teachers whenever the situation suited them.

Peter Montanesi, the middle brother, almost annihilated Mr. Haliak's chemistry lab when he put a cigarette out in a jar filled with a liquid he thought was water. Mr. Haliak (who had been a fencing champion in the Olympic games in the fifties) was amazingly understanding. Instead of piercing Peter with one of the swords he kept on display high on the wall above the blackboard, he grudgingly promised to give him a passing grade if Peter promised never to contemplate a future in science or to accept employment in any job where things were likely to explode.

At any time during the day, the fire alarm would regularly detonate and two thousand students in a casual sort of panic that had become routine, would head for the exits. There were too many fire alarms in Western's endless halls and it was always a mystery which one had been tampered with. It was hopeless trying to settle down two thousand students after a fire alarm. There was never an actual fire, but you could bet there had been a Montanesi next to the fire alarm somewhere in the building. Whenever they were caught for some prank, the brothers never seemed to fear the penalties of their tomfoolery and they accepted their inevitable detentions as a victory and reward, almost enjoying their stopover in the principal's office.

*

The Montanesi brothers were what my mother always referred to as "*imbecilli.*" They were beyond redemption and my mother never failed to remind me of their present and future worthlessness anytime one of them came into her field of vision. There were not enough prayers anyone could deliver that would work their magic of salvation on those boys and she often made the sign of the cross when she saw one of them, partly as insurance for herself and partly because she was superstitious enough to believe in the power of blessings.

"Don't you ever come home with a boy like those *delinquenti*," mother warned me. "Those boys are a wretched curse on their poor mother. Those boys are three deep thorns embedded in her poor broken heart, *povera donna,* poor woman."

But the truth was that their mother adored her three sons just as they were. Mrs. Montanesi walked proud next to her boys, her little five-foot frame waddling next to her three magnificent offspring. Her heart showed no sign of being poor or broken. It beat quite normally on her generously endowed and bouncy chest with all the love she held there for her fine-looking sons. Mrs. Montanesi never missed an opportunity to embrace them when they were in her presence and in public view of neighbours and strangers, never failing to comment on how handsome and precious they were. In the summers when they sat on the front veranda, little Mrs. Montanesi would never tire of bringing them cold drinks and watermelon, planting loud kisses on their heads every time she walked back into the house. When she called out to them from the front porch to come in for dinner she always addressed them as her angels. "*Belli angeli di mamma*, come to eat."

The boys adored her too.

Her boys often alluded that little Mrs. Montanesi was, in many ways, as much of a "ball breaker" as her beloved delinquents. She was energetic, loud, and opinionated in her conversations, but she had a big charitable heart. Erminia Montanesi was a neighbourhood delight, always ready to share her offerings from the garden and her endless cooking tips for every vegetable she grew in her back yard. When she shared the best of her garden, she often had a raunchy joke or story to accompany the gift, which always resulted in a burst of loud and uncontrollable laughter. She didn't really care whether people in the neighbourhood liked her or not, whether they found her loud or distasteful. The little mother seemed as secure in who she was as her boys were. If she had to yell out an insult or a compliment to anyone, at anytime, including to her sons, she did so without a second thought. Her sons were her treasures. She took their side in any confrontation, faithful to the bone, proud of every single hair that grew on their mischievous heads.

Erminia Montanesi showed slightly less appreciation for the quiet and solitary Mr. Achille Montanesi, her husband of twenty-seven years. Mr. Montanesi spent most of his evenings in the garage he had turned into a workshop, surrounded by stacks of wood and the various materials he had piled in corners, brushes and cans of paint, and jars of assorted nails. He always seemed to have a hammer in his hand and he continually puffed away on Export "A"s. My family lived across the street and I often heard him, no matter the season or weather, the garage door open, the one light bulb shining and a radio faintly playing what seemed a jazzy kind of music as he hammered away, nailing something together and banging something else into shape. Some evenings when the radio was silent you could hear him whistling some lovely tunes. He could whistle for long periods as he moved about in his garage. Sometimes my father, who would sit on the veranda at night to smoke his cigarette, would recognize the tune Mr. Montanesi was whistling and he'd join in. But my father wasn't a good whistler. At a certain hour little Mrs. Erminia Montanesi would come out to the porch and shout out to her husband, "Achille ... Achille ... time to come inside." The hammering would stop. The whistling would stop. The light would go off.

*

The chair outside the principal's office always had a Montanesi brother slumped into it. Mr. Rayner had become so familiar with them that during a morning assembly he once offered to take the brothers home with him during summer vacation, so he wouldn't miss their daily visits. He had become so schooled in their behaviour that he seemed almost charmed by their constant impertinence. The summers would be a respite for Mr. Rayner and the lull was a welcome relief for the teachers and the staff at Western Technical and Commercial High School.

There wasn't much to do in the summers unless you had a summer job. Most of us found part-time work in grocery stores and variety stores, others were taken into the factories where our parents worked and spent the summers in hot and stuffy buildings doing small jobs like packing, folding, labelling boxes, and other similarly mundane tasks. If you didn't find a summer job, you pretty much hung around the park. The Montanesi brothers had part-time jobs on weekends at the local hardware store and pumping gas at Scotty Campbell's gas station, but they spent most of their summers at Earlscourt Park and in the back lanes by Lansdowne Avenue and along the railway tracks by Caledonia. Mrs. Montanesi always packed three paper bag lunches stuffed with fruit and sandwiches and set the brothers free in their summer playground while she and her husband both went off to work at York Steel. The park was everyone's playground, it was all we had, all we could afford for the summer break, and while some of us would head over to Harvey's for burgers and fries, the Montanesi boys would sit under a tree and unpack their paper bags. Between soccer and baseball and racing up and down the railway tracks, they would eat their packed lunch, then strip down to their shorts and lie on the grass smoking cigarettes and playing cards. On their way home from work, Mr. and Mrs. Montanesi would pick them up in their green Volkswagen van and they would all head home together. Little Mrs. Montanesi must have thought her boys would be safer out in the park where there was plenty of space for them to run around, than they would be at home. After all, there was not much damage you could do to the park.

*

Nick Montanesi took my breath away. He made my heart flutter every time his beautiful body moved anywhere where my eyes could see him. Nick was the oldest of the brothers. Big, bad Nick with the Elvis mane that hung over his eyes,

filtering the fire
that germinated
from deep in his soul.

Nick made me want to write very bad, bad poetry.

Nick with the cool Ray-Bans down his nose and a smile that could send you to confession. Nick, whose Polish girlfriend, Barbara, wore miniskirts up to her pretty little round ass, and whose long, straight golden hair seemed too blonde to be real, but it was. He called her Bashu. I called her something less kind. Bashu was everyone's dream girl, the prettiest, the sweetest, the body of a young goddess, the girl who made everyone's eyes turn to look at her. It was easy to see why Nick was in love with her.

Nick was a walking, talking cliché of everything I should have disliked about certain kinds of boys. The boys we all yearn and lust for but often pretend to reject. He was too good looking, too cool to ever look at me, the girl across the street who had none of Bashu's charms. I had just turned sixteen the year Nick broke my heart, but he never, ever knew it.

*

Adamo slid into the front seat of my row, turned to his audience and then to me, and winked his introduction with that tempting half smile. I couldn't believe that he'd even noticed me, irrelevant first year in high school me, grade nine me. It was all I could do not to stand up and take a bow in front of the class. I turned my face to the window and let the blood fill my cheeks. Every time he turned to tease me, I was struck by his soft and clear eyes in that beautiful, empty, oversized head of his, and those lips that could probably never spell a word with more than two syllables. He had lips that curled at the end when he smiled, as if they wanted to be kissed. I looked at Adamo and saw the lips of his big brother Nick.

As Mr. Bow-Tie Yaborski chalked assignments on the blackboard, oblivious to anything in class, Adamo turned to me. "Hey, Suzy baby, wanna play with me after school?"

"The name is Agnes," I said.

"Holy shit! Agnes? What kinda name is that?"

"It's my name, so what?"

"Sounds like a grandmother name. You ain't my grandma are you, Agnes?" His brown eyes with the thick lashes flirting as they stared directly into mine.

"I'll ask my grandmother if she wants to come and play with you."

"I like you Agnes. Come out and play with me. I need someone to play with."

His charisma was impossible to resist and I couldn't help but smile.

"That's my Suzy Agnes baby, you like me. I can see you do."

"Take it easy, Casanova." I said.

"Casa Loma? No way, Suzy Agnes, baby. Casa Loma is way

too far. I'll meet you at the Tivoli after school. Be there. Don't break my heart."

He turned to face Mr. Bow-Tie whose chalk marks had listed a dozen rules on the black slate. I examined the back of his head where the subtle brown curls landed on his shirt collar and stared for the longest time. Adamo Montanesi had asked me to go out and play and I really, really wanted to go.

The Tivoli was a greasy spoon by St. Clair and Dufferin where everyone hung out after school, everyone except the "niners." Sometimes the students from Oakwood Collegiate ventured in, but they looked down their noses at the Tech and Commercial students who were destined to be less than the academic wizards they felt themselves to be, so they didn't mix much with those of us who might be future car mechanics or lowly secretaries.

The Tivoli reeked of hormones, cigarette smoke, and the stench of french fries and onion rings. Saturated into every corner of the grimy place was that unmistakable and everlasting smell of fried oil. The booths with the fake red leather seats were faded and worn, and the tables covered with yellow plastic laminate were dotted with cigarette burns. The Tivoli was the Montanesi brothers' Palais Royale. They were there every day after school, and they sat in the same booth popping quarters in the juke box, eating oily fries and lemon pies, and drinking cokes on ice. Rock and Roll was still the rage and Elvis was still king, but England had given us the Beatles and the Rolling Stones and all of a sudden the Montanesi boys had to relinquish the juke box to some different sounds.

That year the Montanesi brothers were flying high and I wanted to go along for the ride, to be part of their magic, to be the girl they desired. I wanted to be their Anne Margret, their Jane Asher, or their Marianne Faithful, so I headed to the Tivoli with my binder pressed to my chest and my hair teased stiff, too much Tigress perfume on my skin and Mary Quant on my lips. I was ready for my initiation into the slippery den of after school temptation. This would be the day that Nick Montanesi would set eyes on me, the girl from across the street, the new beauty in grade nine, the destined love of his life. I was sure he could not help but fall victim to my Tigress charms and he would forget Bashu and become mine forever.

I walked to the Tivoli, paused at the door, and looked inside. There they were. As I opened the door, Adamo saw me and called out, "Hey, Suzy Agnes baby, I knew you couldn't stay away. Come and park your sweet *bon-bon* right here next to mine."

He smiled and motioned me over. That's when Nick looked up and for a few seconds his brown and green speckled eyes, gems that they were, belonged to me. If the world existed at all in those few seconds it had completely stopped. All I saw was Nick's brilliant, unblemished and beautiful face looking directly at me. I forgot who I was, where I was, what language I spoke. I had no quick lines, no witty introductions, I simply stood a petrified Tigress smelling, hair-teased, red-lipped grade niner, frozen at the entrance of the Tivoli Restaurant just as Bashu's little round ass pushed by me, bouncy, bouncy toward the sacred booth.

"Out of my way, niner!" Bouncy, bounce, she brushed past me.

I watched Bashu slide her perfect bottom next to Nick and cuddle him close. She pulled his magnificent face to hers and opened his mouth with her tongue and the lips did the rest. Nick was hers. The spell broke. I could feel my knees lose their poise and I took a deep breath and turned around to leave. As

I walked away, Adamo's voice shouted out to me again, "Hey Suzy Agnes baby, where you going? Come on over here!"

I opened the door and walked out.

"Come back, Suzy Agnes baby, come back and play with me. I need someone to play with." I could hear Adamo's voice through the glass door but I never turned around.

It was rare that Adamo made the nine o'clock homeroom class, but when he did I kept a safe distance having moved myself to the opposite side of the room as far from his desk as possible. I was not ready for the Montanesi brothers, not Adamo or Nick, and my Tivoli experience had proven that. I tried to steer my heart toward a goal that had nothing to do with romance, but I was sixteen, and life was all about romance.

*

That same year, just after Christmas, our family moved to a new house in Downsview. It was the brand new split-level dream home that my mother had always wanted, at Keele and Wilson, on a street with lots of driveways, no laneways, and no trees. I left the old neighbourhood, Western Tech and Commercial, the Tivoli, and the Montanesi brothers behind. My new Catholic high school had an invasion of immigrant girls in blue uniforms and sensible shoes. No distractions or greasy spoons or bad boy brothers to mess with the heart. I studied hard. After high school, I went to York University, got a degree in Education, began a teaching career, and married a gentle, hard-working man who ran his own hardwood flooring business. We raised two children. Life was pleasant.

I carried Nick inside my head for the longest time but it was Bashu who eventually married him. They had three kids. After high school, Adamo went out west to Calgary for many years, made a fortune, charmed a couple of Prairie girls but never married. Peter never took chemistry again but opened his own paint and wallpaper stores that were a smashing success. He met a woman who worked as an interior decorator, and fell in love. My mother kept me informed and up to date with the brothers' lives because she stayed in touch with little Mrs. Montanesi after we moved away. Their regular phone conversations would be filled with little Mrs. Montanesi's news about her beautiful and brilliant boys and all their accomplishments. In time, my mother, who had always been less than appreciative of the boys, had softened her opinion of them. When we all saw each other again it was at little Mrs. Montanesi's funeral many years later, when I dutifully accompanied my mother to the viewing. It did not matter that decades had passed and that the friendship between them had continued simply through telephone conversations. My mother's deep respect and cultural sense of duty were her doctrine, and her friendship was sincere. I, as usual, was the one who accompanied my mother to her various obligations. This time I went without complaint.

My mother entered the funeral home ahead of me. I followed closely behind, watching her steps, keeping a safe distance. My mother was a proud woman and would not lean on me. She wanted to walk independently as she scrutinized the room looking for Mr. Achille Montanesi whom she spotted immediately. Mr. Achille Montanesi, who had long ago put away his hammer and had for many years quit smoking Export "A"s, looked small in his dark suit with the black tie. He sat quietly, surrounded by his many grandchildren. I stood at the back entrance of the large room that was bright and overpowering with the mixed fragrances of too many flowers. While my mother made her way toward Mr. Achille to offer condolences, I looked around to see whom I recognized. My heart laboured a moment as my eyes landed on Nick Montanesi sitting in the front row by the casket. My breath stopped in my throat. Nick had lost his Elvis Presley mane but not his incredible cheekbones. His face had succumbed to sadness but not to time. He was still beautiful. He was still Nick. Bashu's round little ass had grown quite wide, spilling over the sides of the chair, but there she was, sitting next to Nick as close as she had in that booth at the Tivoli that September so long ago, holding his hand as tenderly as if she were still eighteen.

Peter was standing, tanned and elegant in his double-breasted grey suit next to his thin, stunning wife. They were smiling and shaking hands with visitors. I looked around to see if I could spot Adamo, the only brother who had ever spoken to me. Standing by a tall vase of white roses, I noticed his profile by his mother's casket. He was straight, determined, his hands folded as if in prayer. I moved closer so I could see his face. Those still clear, soft eyes were swollen. He had kept all that beautiful hair though it was now evenly layered with fine white strands. It still fell in curls around his collar the way it had way back then. When I approached him and said hello he smiled politely, his lips still curled at the ends. I knew from the way he looked at me that he didn't remember me. I put my arms around him and hugged him for the very first time. I felt the strength I knew was always there.

Adamo had not lost that natural charm. It was there in the way he looked at me, in the understated way he held my hand and thanked me for coming to pay respect to his mother. How different his approach from that first day in high school. Then he asked my name. I felt the same flutter in my heart that I had felt the day the door swung open and he strutted into Mr. Bow-Tie's classroom at Western Tech and Commercial High.

"My name is Ascenza," I said, with a half smile. "But I used to be Suzy Agnes Baby, once upon a time."

➳ THE APRON ⬻

I learn from her how a woman is made for love
and for cleaning house.
—Mary Di Michele, "Mimosa"

BETTINA HAD ALWAYS BEEN THERE; he could not remember a time without her. She had been a little less bent in the past, her hair thicker, less white than it had now become, and he remembered how much quicker her steps had been in the old house on Shanly Street. Up and down those cellar stairs fetching and carrying what she needed from the chilled *cantina*. The stairs were never a challenge. She climbed them easily, never holding on to the banister. She would effortlessly make her way up the steep steps, her arms filled with jars, bottles, and cans. Up and down a dozen times a day in that cellar where she did the washing and where she ironed and folded load after load of the family's laundry. Bettina always made sure the freezer that occupied part of the cellar was well crammed with dozens of plump chickens, rabbits, and bushels of red peppers she had roasted and prepared in the fall. In winter she would add dozens of fresh links of sausage that Andy, her grandson, had helped to make. His job was to tie each link with a thick string and then, with a large needle, he would prick tiny holes into the casings. That cellar was a palace of tasty things and the house on Shanly Street was a good place to live.

Andy knew Bettina was home whenever he opened the door and the tempting smell of tomato and garlic simmering on the stove welcomed him home from school. He knew Bettina best by the delicious scents she released through the house as she stood, for hours, cooking on that old gas stove next to the window that looked on to the long, rectangular garden as she sang one of those songs with words he didn't understand. There wasn't a day he would not come home to a house overflowing with tempting aromas that settled in his nostrils and made him feel hungry and safe.

The Victorian house on Shanly Street was tall and perhaps a little tight, with small but comfortable rooms. The family always ate in the kitchen at the table with the six chairs that Bettina's husband Gaetano (who had been a fine carpenter), had built and varnished with his own hands. The table was strong and solid, made from oak.

"It will last forever," Bettina would say.

Andy sat next to Bettina and she'd make sure he'd eat every morsel on his plate. Sometimes she'd wipe his mouth, he was only six or seven then and it was quite all right for her to do that still. After supper she would leave them to each other, Andy, his mom and his dad, while she prepared her handbag with a few dollars for the collection plate at offertory, her rosary beads and Kleenex. Then she would walk the short blocks south on Dovercourt to Bloor Street to the evening mass at Saint Anthony's Catholic Church. It had been her routine for years, and she never missed a mass if it was at all possible.

Bettina was very content being Andy's grandmother and

caregiver. After a sudden heart attack had taken her husband years ago, being there each day for her grandson, Andy, had given her purpose. After Gaetano died Bettina had left her job at Reliable Toy Company. She had worked in the windowless factory for over twenty-five years packing and checking toys for imperfections. She had worked on that production line with other women who spoke Greek or Portuguese or Italian, blaming her lack of English on the fact that in that factory they spoke every language but English. She often reminisced about those days. They had been hard but they had been good, productive years.

Saint Anthony's church offered her a place to go where she could be with others like her who were now retired and well into their final decades. The evening mass was attended mostly by widows and widowers, a few homeless who came in for the warmth, and perhaps by some who weren't fortunate enough to have someone like Andy to love and to cook for. The regulars who met each evening had developed a friendly and communal relationship. They seemed to share much in common and their hours together were not only about prayer. They would meet at the church each weeknight and sometimes twice on Sunday when they would gather for special events. Often the occasion offered them the opportunity to bake treats that they would share in the basement hall of the church. Bettina was blessed with a good voice and she sang in the choir on Sunday at the Italian mass. It brought her great pleasure to sing the Italian hymns she had learned throughout her life and she sang them with a delightful voice.

After the evening mass Bettina enjoyed the walk down Bloor Street with Mrs. Cardoso and Mrs. De Franco who both lived a few houses up the street from hers on Shanly. On their way home, the three women would stop at the corner Mini Mart or as Mrs. Cardoso called it the *Meno Marta*. Bettina allowed herself a coffee crisp chocolate bar while Mrs. De Franco, who was fond of potato chips, always chose the salt and vinegar ones. Poor Mrs. Cardoso had diabetes so she never indulged in anything sweet and only helped herself to a couple of the potato chips Mrs. De Franco would offer. On their way home to Shanly Street, between their slow steps and their munching, the women would converse and laugh and sometimes Mrs. De Franco led them in a soft rendition of a favourite song. Mrs. De Franco, who also had a lovely voice, could have been a fine singer in another time and another place. In her native city of Naples, she had sung in the church of the *Immacolata* with a choir of youngsters. But during the war the church of the *Immacolata* had been destroyed during an air raid over the city and turned to a mountain of rubble. Mrs. De Franco did not join a choir again until she met Bettina and Mrs. Cardoso on the evenings at St. Anthony's.

Mrs. Cardoso, who had developed her diabetes as a young woman, was always complaining about the lack of sugar in her life. Not only the kind of sugar you ingested through sweets and chocolate bars she would add with a big laugh, knowing she would somehow tickle the "I am embarrassed gene" of her friends. "What are you so shy about? Are you going to tell me all your children were immaculate conceptions?" Mrs. Cardoso would tease her two church pals. Mrs. Cardoso who had a wickedly fun sense of humour, was also a widow who by the age of forty had given birth to seven children and was now the proud grandmother of twelve grandchildren, whom she loved to praise endlessly.

It took longer to get home from St. Anthony's than it did to get there, but the women were fine with that. When they waved their good night they were satisfied that another evening had been lived in grace, with prayer, song, laughter and a sweet and salty treat.

Bettina's day had purpose and even though she missed her husband Gaetano, she had found ways of coping without him. Some days she hardly thought of him at all, keeping busy with Andy, the house, church, and when the spring came around, her endless efforts to keep Gaetano's garden alive. It was in that garden she most treasured the thought of her husband. In that garden she was happy and never felt alone. What more could an old woman want? Her best days were in the past and although she allowed herself moments of nostalgia, she never let herself be controlled by her memories. Nostalgia was dangerous she thought, best kept under control. She made sure never to allow her memories to bring her to a place of sadness or fear. Bettina was content. She could end her days here on Shanly Street. It would be fine, she thought.

Andy had just begun his second grade when his father came home one night and announced to the family that the house on Shanly Street was becoming too old and too small. Andy's father wanted a house with more land. It was time to find a place with lots more space, many more rooms, and much more sky.

Andy was too young to protest and his mother agreed with whatever Andy's father wanted. Bettina really had no say at all even though the house on Shanly Street was the only house she had ever lived in since 1959, when she had married Gaetano. When her husband died, the house on Shanly Street had become hers, but she had signed it over to her son the very day that Andy was born.

Bettina knew every inch of the Victorian house, every mouse hole and spider web. She had scrubbed every cupboard, every corner, every stair. She had raised her two children there, tended a garden, and loved her husband in that house on Shanly Street that had suddenly become too small. There were trees she had planted with Gaetano that were fully grown now. There were plants in the garden that she had cared for as she had cared for her own children; they would need attention still. And now the house had become too small, too old and without sky.

Andy finished the second grade at St. Anthony's Catholic school on Shanly Street. Bettina had walked her two boys to the school back in the 1970s and now she walked Andy there every morning and waited for him every afternoon. The building had been renovated and now the large windows and bright round foyer with the multi-coloured tiles was quite a change from the practical and unadorned original. The school was modern and colourful and the children enjoyed their new playground with shiny new equipment to climb and jump on. Andy loved his school and went happily, skipping beside his grandmother every morning without fuss. That July Andy turned eight. That July they made the move.

The new house was truly brand new. It was just as Andy's father had promised: a big house with many rooms and land as far as she could see, acres of it, all theirs, all open, empty and full of sky. It could have been someone's paradise. Andy's mom and dad busied themselves in making it pretty and comfortable and serene. A wrought iron fence with locked gates went all around the property. Andy helped his father dig holes and plant fruit trees and bushes and perennials. Bettina knew she would not have enough time to see the trees bear their fruit.

Andy started his third grade in a new school named after a prime minister and not a saint. He was quite the independent boy in his third grade and he enjoyed being picked up each morning in a brand new yellow school bus. There was no sidewalk around the new house and the school with the prime minister's name was many kilometres away so Bettina could not walk Andy there. She watched and waved as Andy climbed into the big shiny vehicle at eight-fifteen every morning and then she'd retreat to the elegant finished basement where she would dial the phone numbers of Mrs. Cardoso and Mrs. De Franco hoping to share long talks, but often they were not available. It was rare she would catch them before their walk down Bloor Street to the church and it was always too late on their return to bother them and sometimes she let the moment pass and the phone calls would be postponed. The days seemed longer in the big new house even if there were more stairs to climb and more furniture to dust. Bettina kept busy with her usual chores and sometimes just before she would begin to cook, waiting for Andy to return on the yellow bus, she would treat herself to a coffee crisp chocolate bar before she tied her apron around her. When Andy opened the door each day, Bettina's cooking waited for him, the aromas were the same, tempting, delicious, and he knew he was home and all was fine.

It was January, half way through his third grade year, when the snow was so high and the roads icy, that the school bus was cancelled and Andy spent some days watching Bettina create the dishes he loved to eat. Around Andy's little belly Bettina would tie her favourite apron, the one with the image of a chef wrapped in strings of sausages. Andy and Bettina were happy in the kitchen on snowy days in January, mixing ingredients, concocting brilliant meals with delectable aromas and tasty treats as she sang those songs that Andy didn't understand.

"When did you learn how to cook all this stuff, *Nonna*?"

"Long, long time ago, *bello mio*, when I was more small than you, but not in a nice kitchen like this one."

"Why, didn't you have a kitchen when you were small?"

"We no have such nice things when I was small like you. No big stove, no big fridge. But my mamma made good things from what we have."

"You have them now, so it's okay." Andy smiled, as he stirred the big bowl of cake batter.

Bettina wished it would snow without end and that Andy could remain eight forever, but the snow melted and Andy went eagerly back on the yellow bus to his new school.

One Friday afternoon in late March the yellow bus dropped Andy off at the gate where Bettina often waited for him. She wasn't there. The late winter sky offered a bitter chill and Andy hurried to the front door anxious to get inside. The door was unlocked. Strange for the door to be unlocked, Andy thought, but he walked in without concern. But there was nothing in the air to greet him. Nothing warm or delicious was floating about the large space in the foyer. No steam was rising from the stove in the basement kitchen. No sounds or strange words being sung. He called out for Bettina as he took off his boots and then abandoned his jacket and backpack on the round carpet. Again Andy called out for his grandmother. His voice bounced in the silent calm of the large house with the high ceilings. He called out one more time. Still there was no answer. Reluctantly Andy started down the coiled wooden stairs that led to the kitchen. As he reached the second last step he took hold of the railing with both hands and suddenly stood frozen.

Only a shattering sound leaped from his throat, rebounding against the walls of the large house.

Andy would not be welcomed home in the usual way anymore. Bettina had left him a brand new memory. She had left him a ritual that would replay in his head forever. A ceremony without warmth, or fragrance, or sound, would inhabit his young eyes and creep into his dreams every night for a very long time. Bettina's slight, bent body, a dark single ornament suspended in the unscented basement of the immense new house. Her well-used aprons roped in tight knots around her lithe old neck.

MY FIRST AMERICAN CANDY

And you, my father, there on that sad height,
Curse, bless, me now with your fierce tears.
—Dylan Thomas, "Do Not Go Gentle into That Good Night"

THE FIRST TIME I SAW MY FATHER I thought he would be a big man. I thought he would be wearing an elegant suit with thin stripes and a tie with red polka dots. I thought he'd have on shiny brown shoes made of leather like the ones the rich men wore every day and not only on Sundays or feast days. He would be like the men who smelled of sweet cologne when you stood next to them in church. The men in our town my grandmother called, *i signori*. Fancy men with money in their pockets who wore fine starched hats they charmingly tipped to the women they encountered. The men with thin mustaches that curled at the ends and hair smoothed down with sticky *brillantina*.

These were the men who never chewed tobacco but smoked cigarettes with filters and sometimes lit fat smelly cigars as they gulped down their coffee while standing at the bar in the town's cafes. In the mornings they would sit and read newspapers. In the afternoons they would sit and argue about what they had read that morning. They complained endlessly about the state of the country and those who were in charge of its fate, particularly the corrupt politicians and the thieving priests. They always paid for their coffee with paper bills and never looked at the change. Every day they lounged with their legs crossed, elbows on the tables, as if they owned all the tables and all the chairs in the world and could sit in them forever.

"*Quelli si che sono signori,*" Grandma would say whenever she saw them in the piazza or sitting outside the bars wasting away the hours. Grandma stared with a disapproving envy whenever she saw them parading beside their tittering women on the bridge over the river Liri on Sunday afternoons. They strolled back and forth over that bridge as if they hadn't a care in the world, as if life were one slow walk beside a young pretty, giggling girl on a Sunday afternoon.

I thought my father would be like those men. My handsome father would be strong, rich, and very tall. When we would meet, I imagined he would pull my mother into his embrace and their lips would connect in the longest and warmest kiss ever kissed by anyone. And when the kiss was done, he would turn to my sister and to me, reach into his pockets and scoop out sweet delicious candies that would spill from his hands like miniature lumps of gold.

I couldn't wait to meet the man who was my father waiting for me, for us, in America, with his pockets full of candies. My father in his shiny new brown shoes would be waiting for us in his big red Cadillac. A car like the ones we saw in the American movies with the long pointy fins and the great big doors with silver handles, soft seats, and a radio that played American songs. We would all sit in the big Cadillac eating our candies and then my father would drive us to our American house with a refrigerator, a television, an electric stove, and a warm wool carpet. It was all waiting for us. My father and the American house he had come to prepare during all those years when he was gone, was waiting for us.

Then my father would take us to the American store. The stores I had heard about with the stairs that moved up and down. My father would buy us dresses with matching shoes and he'd buy Mamma a fur coat and a hat like the American ladies wore in the cold and snowy American winters. Mamma would wear gloves to match her purse. My sister and I would wear gloves, too. That's the way it would be once we got to America. Then we would be happy forever.

But my father was not a big man, not big at all. He did not have a mustache and he did not wear a fancy suit or a tie. He was just a man. Not short or tall, an ordinary man with black hair neatly combed with only a hint of *brillantina* smoothing down the strands behind his ears. His shoes did not shine. They were well used and black. He wore a white shirt tucked into plain grey pants and a pack of cigarettes stuck out of his shirt pocket. He didn't look like the fancy men at all. I remember only that his hands had long fine fingers and his nails were cut short. His young face was beardless and his dark eyes were a little sad with the corners down and the lids heavy.

I also remember wondering why his eyes looked so sad. Maybe he was born with sad eyes the way I was born with the mole on my neck. Grandma used to say that sad people were born under the wrong star; maybe my father was one of those who had been born under the wrong star. All I know is he lived the next twenty-three years and his eyes did not change and he never once drove a red Cadillac.

When I first saw my father it was a hot night in June 1960. He was one of many fathers who waited among the crowd gathered at Union Station in Toronto. My sister and I were holding on to Mamma's skirt as she lugged two suitcases down from the train and then down a dozen steep stairs into the crowded waiting area. That night the train station had the feel of a market place, although there was nothing to buy. There were groups of tired, noisy people everywhere. Scattered in every direction, scared and confused faces, familiar faces; something in the shape, the texture of their skin, all too familiar. The scent that hung in the air felt intimate and stifling. I looked around. Had we made it? Was this America?

His walk towards us was slow, as if his legs were heavy to lift. He stopped a short distance away looking curiously at my mother. He stood motionless, unsure what to do. Gradually he resumed walking toward us and when he reached my mother he stopped,staring into her tired face for what seemed an endless time. Neither of them spoke. Only their eyes fixed on each other.

My sister's impatient and curious voice broke the stillness. "*E tu chi sei?*"

My father seemed to snap from his trance and bent down to where his sad eyes fell into my sister's inquisitive stare. "*Sono tuo Papà.*"

Marta didn't care. "*E le caramelle? Dove sono le caramelle?*"

He had remembered the candies. In years to come, he would always remember the candies. His face began to relax as he searched his pocket and out came assorted little lumps wrapped in glittery papers. Marta reached for them and began tearing away at the crinkly treasure. It was then my father turned to me and reached into the other pocket. He pulled out his hand and opened it with a slight tremor and there resting in the fine skin of his palm were three large nuggets wrapped in silver tissue. He reached for me and with his slightly quivering fingers placed the three nuggets in my cupped and waiting hands.

"Ciao, Teresina. Sono Papà."

I felt for the first time the touch of this stranger's hand, this stranger who was my father. As I unwrapped one of the nuggets and placed it in my mouth, I watched him take my mother in his arms and kiss her awkwardly, as if he had forgotten how it was done. He held her very close while Marta and I delighted in our treats. The sugary lumps in my mouth were chewy and melted slowly. I remember thinking that it was the sweetest candy I had ever tasted. My first American candy I later learned was maple caramel and made in Canada.

⇝ WAITING FOR A MIRACLE ⇜

Recalling the always present paradise
We enter and cannot remain in.
—James K. Baxter, "Moss on Plum Branches"

ANGELA MARIA SAT ON A three-legged wooden stool waiting for the cow to pee. Undisturbed in her orb of darkness, she sat in the month of March in the winter of 1951, waiting for Celestina to release her first warm morning brew. Draped around Angela Maria's strong straight shoulders was a black shawl that had by now seen countless winters and at her feet the aluminum pail stood in attendance. Her confident body, heavy with the need of sleep, breathing in the chilled sweetness of hay around the barn.

Celestina's very first morning pee, warm and fresh was what she needed. The very first pee was the healing one. Angela Maria was a woman of faith. She believed in God, believed in the power of miracles, and she had a particular affection for the hard-working saints, especially Saint Anthony. But Angela Maria was also a practical country woman who had considerable trust in the efficient and no-nonsense usefulness of cows. She knew without a doubt that sometimes even the good Lord needed a little help to get the job done.

From the deep pocket of her skirt Angela Maria pulled out the tenant rosary that lived there, and twisted the beads around her fingers, then, while resting the lids of her grey eyes, she began to pray. Prayer was always essential. Rosary beads had a certain presence in moments of required interventions. Rosary beads were often influential on occasions when natural logic seemed to fail. The ones in her hand had been blessed by the *Monsignore* of Pontecorvo back in 1944, during a mass for the fallen soldiers and souls of the departed. The beads were well used and had served her faithfully over the years and she knew they would help her in this circumstance. She also prayed her toes would not turn numb from the dampness and cold, and that March would not behave as delinquently as it had in previous years. March —a selfish and unpredictable month — you never knew what it would bring, a crazy month.

"*Marzo pazzo. Ave Maria, piena di grazia. Amen.*"

Angela Maria was no stranger to the cold. She knew full well it was not much warmer inside the stone walls of her little house. The dampness that lived there had long ago moved to the inside of her bones, but she also knew that Arduino's feet entangled with hers beneath the heavy wool blankets would continue to keep the blood circulating. Arduino with his gigantic arms and hands would surround her body and pull her towards him, his tobacco flesh welcoming and tempting. Arduino would have to wait.

Angela Maria's fingers moved from bead to bead with a hurried tempo as her lips mumbled a sequence of mysterious Latin words before each Ave Maria. Words she had learned but did not completely understand. Her eyelids still resting over her grey eyes, she waited and prayed until the cow was ready to empty her bladder. Celestina was Angela Maria's pride and joy, bought at the *mercato* in Frosinone, a healthy, beautiful calf. She grew into a fine cow that produced plenty of milk for the fresh *ricotta* and cheeses that Angela Maria prepared each day.

Celestina's legs began shifting as she munched away, grinding the hay into a tasty mush. Suddenly her tail jerked from side to side and Angela Maria skipped the third and fourth bead in her hand, eager and ready to receive this marvel about to escape between Celestina's colossal thighs. The beads went back in her pocket and she sat up listening and watching for the next sign. Celestina was about to relinquish her gift.

The March wind had begun whimpering and through the cracks of the barn walls she could see bony slivers of sky. Dawn crept in quietly as a gradual trickling began and Celestina started to move. In the stillness, Angela Maria could hear the melodious sound of a sluggish little fountain and she launched into action. Grabbing the pail she positioned it where she could collect the most liquid as it started to gain momentum, cascading between the cow's legs, a steamy foaming waterfall. The warm, frothy spill of yellow pee drummed into the pail with an intended accuracy. Celestina had been particularly full that morning and the aluminum pail spilled over.

"Brava vacca, brava vacca!"

Angela Maria's hand slapped Celestina's massive backside in a grateful gesture, then she wrapped her shawl tightly around her shoulders and securing it to the waistband of her skirt, and pushed open the barn door. March bit into the morning like a crisp apple, the late winter sky pale and buttery over the countryside. The air sharp in her nostrils, Angela Maria picked up the pail and made her way to the stone house. She was eager to warm her hands by the fire, ready for coffee and a slice of bread and cheese, but not before she had brought Celestina's gift to my bedside. Angela Maria was coming to wake me. She was coming with a full pail of magic from the bladder of her one cherished cow on this shrill March morning, coming to wake me and to heal me.

I was brand new, only two months into my first year. I slept safe in my mother's arms, away from the tart breath of the crazy month, cuddled and warm in Mamma's bulky bed on a lumpy mattress stuffed with cornhusks and wool. My mother's first born; five kilos of dark and soft female flesh, with charcoal eyes and a round bald head. No ordinary round bald head, but one that was covered with dry, cracked and discoloured skin. My mother's treasured first child cursed with a hairless, lumpy, crusty skull, needing a miracle to cleanse it to its natural state.

What was this disease? Nothing a doctor could cure if a doctor could be found. Was it perhaps the result of the evil eye, the envy of a greedy neighbour or a jealous relative? Or was it the mark of a sin never confessed, the result of an abandoned passion, a desire that should never have been? Whatever the cause, whatever the sin, Angela Maria was intent on finding a remedy.

My mother was barely in her twenties, beautiful and ignorant of any sin, her confused youthful face pained with worry. I slept serenely, oblivious to any act of evil or kindness. I could not see my crusty head, could not see the panic I represented. I slept well in Mamma's arms, sin and guilt not yet a presence in my vulnerable and innocent body.

Angela Maria opened the door and marched in, a warrior on a mission, bucket in one hand and clean monogrammed cotton towels in the other. The towels she had collected over the years had been my mother's valued *corredo,* her hope chest, part of her dowry.

"*Svegliati, Antonia!*"

Mamma's sleepy, tired eyes widened as she handed me over to the priestess. On the fresh towel naked and defenseless I lay as Angela Maria searched her deep pockets and her faithful beads reappeared. She placed the crucifix between her fingers and let it travel the length of my body, rested it on my forehead, muttered some words, made the sign of the cross, and then lifted the pail onto the wooden dresser as she cupped her hand and dipped it into the fresh warm pee. My mother watched as Angela Maria held me with one hand while with the other she poured Celestina's brew over the encrusted skin and rubbed it gently, massaging the tepid liquid into my little cranium until it was as marinated as a tender cabbage. She repeated this action several times that morning. When she was certain she had performed the ceremony in abundance to initiate the required miracle, she wrapped a linen towel into a baby turban on my well-saturated little scalp and handed me back to Mamma.

"*Ecco fatto. A domani.*"

For the next six days Angela Maria repeated the ritual. Each morning my tiny head was immersed in Celestina's fresh morning pee. On the seventh day, she and my mother were eyewitnesses to the miracle. They rested. The round scalp of my melon head was beautifully smooth, cleansed free of sin. There was no scar, no scaly skin or residue, nothing left to suggest trespasses of any kind. God and the cow had collaborated well.

Angela Maria did not take miracles lightly. She was well aware that there would be other times, other evil eyes to monitor, perhaps even a sin or two to atone for, so she prayed each morning by the bed my mother and I shared. For the next seven days she would appear at the same hour and murmur her words of indemnity. Her barely audible voice prayed for the absolution of my original sin, for the distancing of any unwelcome and insincere compliment that lurked in jealous hearts. She prayed that envy would never settle anywhere near our home and hearts. She also remembered to give thanks for Celestina's magnificent bladder.

That year March had "come in like a lion" as my grandmother would say, and "gone out like a lamb," taking with it the memory of my tainted head. Spring brought the promise of everything new, fresh and bright as the yellow mimosa in bloom. My proud mother, with me in her arms, warmed by the modest sunshine, strolled up the country road toward town. She would stop at every opportunity to allow neighbours to feast on the treasure I was.

"*Che bella bambina,*" the townsfolk would say. "What a beautiful child."

"Yes, she is beautiful, and look, her head is pink and fuzzy as a peach and as sweet as a ripe persimmon in December," Mamma would answer. It is true my mother was aching with pride for her first born.

My grandmother Angela Maria, who had mothered eight children of her own, was a natural teacher, wealthy in practical wisdom and strength. In the years to come, I learned much by listening to her stories that overflowed with wonder and mystery and that filled me with curiosity, stories from the bible or from legends told and re-told. They spoke of the traditions she practiced, the rituals I learned to honour and respect. By the time I was six years old, my grandmother had begun to share with me all that she knew about the world, the ways of men, women and God. The skills she shared were always those practiced only by women, the ones that mattered, she would say. She taught me that the ways of women were always much harder than the ways of men or God.

On our evening walks to church in the town's piazza, my grandmother wore her long skirt with the deep pockets and the woollen shawl that fell to her knees. I fit neatly under her arm, no taller than her waist. She would cover me with her cloak as she took hold of my hand with only my tiny legs visible. The rest of me was cocooned in the darkness around her body, warm and safe. I walked without the need to open my eyes, sheltered by her side, eavesdropping on her garbled prayers as we walked the half kilometre to town. My world at her waist, beneath her mantle, was all rhythm and footsteps and musical beads.

Before we reached the town square we always stopped at the edge of the bridge where a small wooden hut, not more than two feet tall, stood in the shadow of the street lamp. In the hut was a clay statue of a Madonna in a faded blue gown. There, under the dim light, the tiny lady seemed almost real. Her clay hands had chipped fingers and the plastic flowers at her feet were dusty and grey but to me she appeared regal and beautiful. She was proudly displayed at the entrance to town where everyone who crossed the bridge could see her. Each time we passed her way my grandmother would pull out a crust of bread from her pocket and place it inside the hut at the feet of the statue. She would greet the stone figure like an old friend. I would peek out from beneath the shawl and gawk at the silent lady with her tiny cracked stone hands drawn together, one of her little fingers completely missing, the sparse faded plastic roses forming a crown on her head. As grandmother laid the bread at the lady's feet she would whisper two words, always the same two words.

"Grazie, Signora."

I never asked my grandmother why she thanked the lady as she left the crust of bread each time we passed by. The mystery of it seemed too important to reveal, the ritual comforting.

There was something about how right it felt being under the shawl in the dark, warmed by her body, protected. How natural it seemed that we should greet the statue with an offering of stale bread and then silently walk away in the night. The way it still feels right after all these years when I think about it or when I hold beads in my hand or hide beneath a warm blanket. How reassuring it feels to have a miniature statue of the lady in the blue gown on my bookshelf, here in my Canadian house, on a downtown street in the city of Toronto where I have lived for as many decades as the rosary. The small statue, her hands whole and folded in prayer, belonged to my mother and it was passed on to me when I chose to live in a house of my own. She rests on the same bookshelf where a photograph of Angela Maria in a silver frame hangs. They both look down on me as I sit at my desk for long hours on mornings and evenings, selecting words to write on a page. They look down on me as I sift through memories that prove I have been here, we have been here, and there are stories to write, to share.

And yes, how completely normal it feels, also, when I reflect on cows whenever my head, without warning, begins to itch and I inevitably have to get up to pee.

IN MY BLOOD

...[L]ooking back, my dreams were full of prisons
—Dionne Brand, "ossuary 1"

EACH DAY I WAKE UP TO the same demon. Large as the day before, the week before, as far back as I can recall. When I close my eyes at night I am convinced that when I awake to a brand new morning, I will be free. I will be in control. There will be no confusion. A newborn me, flawless and strong will rise with the sun. But there he is, each morning, each day, each evening as powerful and as beautiful as ever. It is all I can do to keep a safe distance.

You see, I am mad. Madder than any hatter in any fairytale. Madness is in my blood, so I have been told. My mother's mother was mad, a slightly different insanity than mine but just as efficient in its control. I carry the gene, and while her primitive blood primed her for murder, mine landed me solitary and crimeless on the south side of Queen Street. Not in the modern crazy house recently re-invented in the trendy neighbourhood at the end of Ossington Avenue, where the old 999 Queen Street was once the address for those whose minds played dark games, like mine. Now I am further west, toward Lansdowne, where the odd and the weird are well tossed into the blend of peculiar folk and allowed to roam relatively undisturbed.

Queen and Lansdowne Avenue, where the eccentrics and new unwanted citizens, slightly invisible, can still reign free isn't yet a hipster paradise, but that will come soon enough to displace the broken and the sad. Meanwhile the coffee shops still serve the slightly whacky and exhausted souls. The thrift stores and grocers still accept cash from the pungent and unpolished, even if the transactions are without smiles or pleasantries. I make my home in two rooms above a bike shop, where I live with my beautiful demon, my pills, my books, and my black and white cat.

How mad am I, you may wonder, and how do I know? Simple. I have been told it is so. My mother doubted my wholeness from the beginning. You see, I came out wrong, straight from the start. My legs wanted out before my head, causing her unbearable pain. My exit eventually came from an extensive and serious scar across her belly, which marked her for life. The scar will not allow her to forgive me. If I am to assume my entry into the world came with the absence of joy, I would not be mistaken.

It is no secret that I was not a beautiful baby and that my eyes were frighteningly big, slightly crossed and wide open from the very beginning. The dark hair on my head was too thick and disobedient, and the birthmark that ran from my shoulder down my left arm had a texture that resembled the scales of a fish. Mother was not impressed and most likely regretted having brought such an odd creature into the world. How could she have given life to such an organism? Undoubtedly she hoped, in those first years of my childhood, that I might have a kind of transformation and develop into the radiant child she had wanted and believed she deserved. But with time she came to realize that none of my features would ever be radiant and I would be a constant reminder of something imperfect, and, indeed, it broke her heart.

Everything about me displeased my mother. The radically changing shape of my body, the uneven shoulders, the thin legs and the round belly were an assault to her eyes, an irritation. Perhaps the worst of it was my resemblance to her mother, particularly in the cadence of my voice. But it was the sound of my cries in the nights when sleep was impossible that sent her to her own hushed place where she refused to hear me. The nights my demon would visit and I would call for her, she pretended never to hear. As bad as the nights were, the days were sometimes worse. In the daytime I became invisible. The routines of our lives were mechanical, the feeding, the dressing, the sending off to school, all without much more than the obligatory attention until that one day when she could not refuse to see me. It was a Sunday when she returned with the palms and the Easter lily, and found me in the hallway among the empty bottles, the pills. That day she had to look, had to touch before she dialled the numbers, and they came to remove me from her polished hardwood floors that I had stained with my vomit and blood.

My mother now claims only two offspring, the two handsome ones she paid attention to after I was taken away. The two quiet ones with normal sized eyes and heads that are just right. My brilliant brothers are students of business and law, on their way to success with Mamma's approval and blessings. My brothers are the correct children who bring honour, stability, and respect to our family. My brothers know little about me, only that I exist, and they are not interested in knowing anything more. In this city it is easy to disappear quietly. Families bury you without notices or obituaries and there is no need to leave any history. Mine will go with me.

My father is a foolish man who believes he is smart. Real estate is the religion he practices. He buys and he sells. He rents and banks his profits. He indulges in silk shirts he can afford but cannot wear with any style. His dream of an exclusive membership to a golf club is what he most desires even if he cannot master the game. His annual jaunts to Vegas are an attempt to prove he is a big time player.

My family have erased me. They remain untouched by my existence. They are safe in a gated community, in a house with solar panels on a wide cul-de-sac in the city of Vaughan. The city of Vaughan where there are no forests or mountains or madness, but simply the well-designed illusion of space and country. A modern city constructed and assembled by experts who deal in the retail of deception. Everywhere the presence of greed is chiselled into the beauty of marble and stone. The opulence of vanity well landscaped and neatly maintained. What lurks behind the heavy drapes of silk and velvet is another mystery. But I am mad, madder than a hatter in a fairytale. I have nothing sane to offer; my opinion is irrelevant and immaterial.

This madness I possess will not commit murder but it has been an unpleasant reality for my family. My madness had managed to spoil the orderly meals, interfered with the well-set table my mother always prepared, and she decided long ago she would have no part of my madness at her dinner table, breakfast table, or at any table she would prepare in the future. With that decision she promptly proceeded to wipe clean, with antibacterial wipes, any surface that held traces of my DNA. My mother's first born is ecologically removed from her counter tops and her furniture.

I am mad, madder than any Alice tumbling down a rabbit hole. My mother's mother was mad. So mad she murdered her rival. On a bright clear day without clouds or darkness of any kind, she drowned her rival in the same well where she collected her drinking water. Pushed that young, slender girl with the auburn pigtails without a moment's hesitation, and watched her drop into the bottomless blackness of the stone well. When the water had settled to a still calm she filled her water jug, took a cool drink from the bucket, and walked home unshaken and composed, humming a tune. There would be no competitor, no opponent to lay claim to what she had decided belonged to her. The handsome son of the textile merchant would be hers. That madness is in my blood.

Shall I tell you more about the woman whose blood is in my veins? The woman they called *La Strega di Bojiano* who lived in a hut half way up the mountain behind the Majella. That woman was my mother's mother. Born in that mountain town where our roots are mysterious and mangled. There, where this blood comes from, where my mother's mother lived with her wild heart among the green fingers of gods and devils. Was it the forest, or the mountain? Was it the darkness or the light that gave her the vision and the voices? This I cannot tell you, because I do not know. It might have been all or none. There was never much talk about the reasons. There was never much talk at all. The silence kept us safe, so mother thought. What we did not reveal to anyone, what we did not acknowledge, did not exist. What we did not speak about could not be heard. The new country over an ocean, the new neighbours, the distance from forests and mountains would keep us safe. It was always that silence that brought the beautiful demon to my side.

The auburn pigtails eventually floated to the surface and the beautiful, slight girl, no longer beautiful, was laid to rest in a field where poppies grew in the right season. It was said that after she was found the well dried completely, never to fill with water again, but that may just have been a tale I imagined or dreamed. The son of the textile merchant married the woman who hummed a strange tune and together they left the mountain and headed to the sea where they crossed the ocean on a giant ship to a land that held no history. And child after child, after child, there would come a time, eventually, for me.

My mother's mother offered me her story in a weak moment of clarity between life and death, when madness becomes confession and I was the necessary God she recognized sitting by her side. I listened. I understood the force between us.

She went to her God, believing she'd been forgiven.

At times now I turn to prayer. I foolishly attempt confession. I can remember the Catholic words from school days.

Hail Mary full of grace
the Lord is with thee.
Blessed art thou among women
and blessed is the fruit of thy womb, Jesus.

But I am mad. The prayers will not work for me. I carry too many sins of inheritance before the blood runs clear. I have a legacy I cannot escape. My mother has tried. To escape I mean. But I accept the madness, the mangled roots, the stone well. It is all part of who I am. My mother will have to fill her own water jug one day and carry it the distance. She will have to find her tune to hum, as she too walks away from the well.

Sometimes when the night sneaks up on me and I sit alone, above the bike shop, as endless streetcars rumble past and the lonely voices from the city street rise up to my windowsill, I think about the forest where I have never been. I think about the mountain I have never seen or the full moon that lives inside me. I think about how I came to be above a bike shop, alone, on an ordinary street, in a city where love is often homeless. And sometimes before the demon comes, I imagine that I am Alice plummeting into the rabbit hole, down, down, to the bottom of a soft green meadow where my mother is waiting for me. She recognizes me, beautiful as I am. This time she hears me; she knows it is my voice. She listens.

I close my eyes, I imagine when I wake in the morning my beautiful demon will be gone. The blood will be clean.

PAINTED WINDOWS

The only time my mother is happy
is when she's thinking about being sad!
—Gia Milne-Allan

MAMMA IS CRYING IN HER BEDROOM downstairs. I hear Mamma crying every night since we got here in this tall, dark house with all these stairs, this starved house without sunlight, with windows painted shut. Windows that keep the air out. This house with wooden floors she makes me scrub over and over again with bleach and turpentine. She says she likes the smell. She says it is a clean smell. It makes my hands burn and my skin peel. Mamma isn't worried. She shows me her hands. I guess she knows best.

*

I hate this house on this street where all the women look like my mother. Where all the houses look like each other. I hate the darkness of this house, especially at night. The nights when all I hear is Mamma crying. The nights I can't breathe and want to break all the windows. I'm not sure why Mamma cries. I think she misses *Nonno* and *Nonna*, like I do. Maybe she cries for them. My father is never home. Maybe she cries for him too.

*

My sister Nina is six, but she looks older, except when she sleeps. When she sleeps, she looks like a baby. I watch her sometimes. Her eyes perfectly still, her long, soft lashes resting on her cheeks. She always sleeps with her favourite doll by her side, safe and warm. I watch her little body quiver and rise, listening to her sighs. I watch for a long time when I can't sleep and then I hear Mamma, crying. Every night Mamma's tears fill this dark house. I want to walk down the stairs, open the door to her room, run into her arms, jump into her bed. I want to stop her sadness, sweep up the tears. I want to make everything clean, make it all smell nice. But I can't. I don't know how. So I listen. I look at Nina as she sleeps. I count Mamma's tears. The last one. Silence. Then I fall asleep.

*

On Sunday, Mamma put on a nice blue dress and powder on her face and bright red lipstick. She had bought Nina and me new shoes. We put them on and danced round and round, tap tapping on the wooden floors. Mamma packed a shopping bag with sandwiches and fruit. She took Nina and me to High Park so we could run in the grass and look at the giant maple leaf that was made of flowers. She let us sit by the pond and eat our sandwiches and throw bits of bread to the ducks and the birds. I liked High Park. Liked the long streetcar ride from College Street. Liked watching the city move through the streetcar windows. Watching the sun play hide and seek with the buildings. We counted the traffic lights. We counted the cars and trucks that went by. Happy little girls in shiny new shoes, hand in hand, with a pretty smiling mother wearing bright red lipstick.

*

Three traffic lights before the park the houses begin to change from small plain ones to large beautiful ones. They look a little like castles. Flowers and trees all around. Windows with coloured glass. Open windows. Big, open windows. I stare. My eyes wide open. I want to live there! That one! No, that one, I want to live in that one!

*

My father is home. They're yelling again. His fists hard on the kitchen table, over and over. The words in Italian that make my mother scream. Nina and I huddle together in the same bed. Scared. The slaps echo. They don't stop. Mamma's body against the furniture. We start to cry and hold each other tight. Nobody hears us.

*

Mamma left for work at six. Papa didn't come home last night. Got to get Nina ready. Got to get myself ready and go to school. I'm cold. I want Mamma. I want *Nonna*. I want somebody.

*

Nina burned herself today with boiling water that fell all over her leg. I was cooking pasta for our lunch. She got in my way. She screamed and I screamed too. No one was home. No one heard. I put her in the bathtub and ran cold water over her leg. The skin looked funny. Nina screamed louder. I phoned my aunt. "Butter" she said. "Put butter on it." It didn't seem right. I kept running the cold water, held her hand tight. I kept kissing her wet cheeks over and over. We cried for a long time alone in the bathroom, waiting for Mamma to come home. The doctor said I did the right thing. I was a smart, quick thinking girl. I got hit anyway. Should have been more careful. The scar might stay. Mamma was grateful it wasn't Nina's face. Nina has a beautiful face.

*

Got my period today. It feels awful. Mamma made me stay in bed. She said I could skip school for a few days. She didn't explain why. "Just stay in bed," she said. She came back a little later holding something in her hand. Thick cotton pieces of material folded into a long thick strip. She told me to pin it to my panties with safety pins. Diapers! They looked like diaper pins. "I won't. I don't want to wear this, I don't want to!" I screamed at her. She looked at me with the saddest eyes and then walked out of the room. She left me there with the diaper in my hand. I sat on my bed squeezing the safety pins open and shut.

*

My first Christmas in Canada. I love the bright coloured lights that shine everywhere in the city. I have never seen so many pretty lights, colours that flicker and wink like fireflies in winter. They make me happy. I stare out the window and look at the tall dark houses lit with these magic lights. The pine trees in the front gardens, the verandas, the dry, naked bushes sprinkled with coloured lights. I want lights. I beg Mamma for lights for our window, the one that never opens. But there's no money for lights. No money for unnecessary things. I stare out the window wishing I lived in another house.

*

My aunt and uncle came for Christmas Eve. They came in my uncle's truck, the one he delivers bread with. My cousins are all boys. They were born here. Nina and I don't speak English very well and they make no effort to understand us. They don't speak any Italian. They're boys. They don't really care about us. They play by themselves.

*

Mamma cooked fish. Only fish on Christmas Eve, the *baccalà* stewed in tomato sauce, onions, and raisins. Lots of onions and some black olives that came in a can. Papa likes to help at Christmas and he cooked the spaghetti with anchovies and garlic. I chopped the parsley. My uncle Ettore brought wine, his own homemade wine. Said he can only drink his own, knows what's in it. He poured some for all of us. The kids got a half glass. His boys added ginger ale to fill up their glasses. Nina and I drank the wine without ginger ale. After the food and the wine we all felt good. We laughed at my uncle's stories and his jokes. He told them in Italian and his boys looked bored and played cards. Nina and I laughed till our sides hurt. I watched my father put his arm around my mother. She got up and went to the kitchen to make coffee.

*

My aunt and uncle left just after midnight. The boys climbed into the back of the truck and sat on a blanket. My father went out a little after they left. He came back two days later.

*

January. The lights still shine in the city but they don't seem to have the same magic. They will soon begin to disappear. I will miss them. My nose is pressed against the frozen window watching the growing darkness. The days are so cold. I can't get warm. I can't get Nina up in the morning anymore. She cries for Mamma. Mamma's at the factory. Nina doesn't care about my explanations. She keeps crying. I feed her Cheerios and milk. I dress her. I comb and braid her hair. She wants Mamma. I start to get angry. I shake her a little. She cries even louder, buries her small head in the hood of her jacket. "I want Mamma," she yells. Then she wraps her arms around my waist and holds on.

*

Mamma got a telegram today. *Nonno* died. She fell on the floor, screaming. I tried to pick her up. Nina was trembling and crying out, "Mamma, Mamma, Mamma!" Mamma put her arms around us and sobbed in big gulps. I could feel her chest against my face, warm, wet, and pounding so fast. Suddenly she pushed me away and held onto Nina. I walked around the room trying to think of what to do. Papa wasn't home. I didn't know where he was.

*

I call my aunt. Soon relatives appear at the door. They bring food. They talk in whispers. My mother sits in the corner of the couch. Relatives take turns comforting her. They put their arms around her. They try to feed her. She refuses. She just keeps wailing. My relatives move around the small rooms in careful steps. There is nowhere to go.

*

They all left, late. My aunt is staying over. My mother hasn't moved from the corner of the couch. I put Nina to bed. Papa finally came home. He said nothing. He is standing by the window, a beer in one hand and a cigarette in the other. Mamma and Papa do not look at each other. They seem so far away. I feel far away. I wonder what they are thinking. I squeeze my eyes and they become blurry. I try to imagine them in each other's arms, their faces close together, their cheeks touching, but they never move. I hide in the dark by the stairs. I do not move. We are all like the windows in this dark, tall house, windows that won't open.

MY GRANDMOTHER IS NORMAL

Believe it, what we lost is here in this room
on this veiled evening.

—Eavan Boland, "What We Lost"

"M*A PERCHÉ? WHY, WHY, YOU no get marry? You such a nice girla, nobody wants marry to you?*" That's the standard greeting I get from my grandmother every time I appear at her front door, steel grey and decorated with an assortment of sticker-type pictures of angels and saints, courtesy of her local church, and a Canadian flag, courtesy of the neighbourhood city councillor. They are all carefully pasted to the solid, impenetrable, intruder-proof door of her modest semi-detached, two-storey house on a one way street just east of Ossington Avenue south of Dupont.

My grandmother had always wanted a new crimson door with a bright and shiny gold knob but my mother insisted that it would make an unflattering statement about those who lived in the house and the neighbours would criticize. Red is my grandmother's favourite colour, gold her favourite mineral or metal, Saint Teresa her favourite saint and I am, without a doubt, her most cherished female grandchild.

My mother — her only daughter — is the official Swiss Guard on regular duty now that my grandmother has reached her mid-eighties. She spends most afternoons taking care of grandmother's needs. My mother does the shopping, housecleaning, banking, and other domestic tasks, while my grandmother spends more and more time reconnecting with her Catholic identity, listening to Radio Maria where the Pope is a frequent guest. My grandmother is also fond of reading religious magazines and baking amaretto cookies for the rosary group who meet every first Friday of the month. *Nonna*'s internal clock is set for the daily viewing of the Eucharist on Vision TV, which is often broadcast either in French or Latin. She has become comfortably bi-lingual in the responses, preferring the Latin because it takes her back to the days when she first learned the prayers. When mass is over, she switches to RAI international television broadcast directly from Italy. RAI helps her reconnect with her original language, although she often complains about the offensive nature of some of the modern programming. This phenomenon of spiritual re-birth has happened in the last ten years or so and I imagine it is a preparation and a type of indemnity for the inevitable realities to come. She has, on occasion, tried to lead me toward her spiritual inspiration, wanting me to join in her appreciation of the "holy," but, as much as she tries, I resist with a sincere politeness that seems to appease her. Her indulgence in the utterly mindless programming of RAI International Television is a little more disturbing.

Before I take off my coat or hang up my purse or remove my shoes or even put my arms around her to say hello, my grandmother asks me the same question, which is really less of a question than it is a sad, painful affirmation of my unfortunate state of spinsterhood. My unexploited and unappreciated feminine charms going to waste, as the clock ticks away, are a constant concern for my grandmother, and a very real reason to devote a decade of prayers to my needs every time she says the rosary. That is the reason I visit only on absolutely necessary occasions. Of course, the necessary occasions are a weekly event with the added special stopover on holy days, and the feast day of Saint Teresa when I bring her a dozen red roses. Yes, roses are my grandmother's favourite flowers. My grandmother's name is Teresa.

I love my grandmother and would never entertain the thought of a mockingly smart response to any of her questions — of which there are laundry bags full, each with an undercurrent of my unrealized state of womanhood — but there have been moments when visions of grand-matricide have flashed appetizingly in my head.

I don't know why she keeps asking me the same thing over and over when I am almost optimistic she really knows the answer, but somehow she needs to play this game that allows a certain pretence into the assumed normality of our totally peculiar family. Nothing about my grandmother or anyone else in my familial tribe is normal, but then what is normal? Is there a family in history who can ever claim the honour?

I am fortunate that my grandmother has a wicked sense of humour and she does not take offence when I mimic her questionable sanity as I play charades with her advice, her concerns, and her God. She laughs easily and with a real need to share the joy that is in her. She also embraces me constantly and I have now learned the hugs are not just a demonstration of affection, but a way to get close enough to slip fifty dollar bills into my pockets, just in case.

My grandmother has buried two husbands. I never met either of them because they exited the planet years before I was born while she was still a relatively young, attractive woman. She has been without a man, husband, for over thirty years and for the past twenty-five of those she has filled me in on her theory that it is a very real improbability that decent, honest, and exceptional men exist in this world. She has also assured me that their participation in the universe is overestimated and in most instances completely not necessary. The fact that my grandmother's God is a man never enters the discussion.

Of course, this disdain for the male gender does not apply to her beloved, perfect nephew, my brother, who is her first grandchild, a gemstone, a remarkable young man beyond any imperfection, resembling Michael the good angel and therefore impossible to criticize. He is, for my grandmother, flawless. She has never asked him when he will marry because there is no need for him to marry. Between my grandmother and my mother he has no real need for a wife, except perhaps for sex, and according to my grandmother, he can find that anywhere. The rest of her angel boy's worldly needs are provided by us. The fact that my brother is thirty-five and still living with our parents does not trouble her at all. It is true that my mother still waits for him to come home, launders his clothes, and no matter what the hour, she is prepared to cook whatever his appetite desires. All this is completely acceptable.

This inevitable contradiction in my grandmother's character and behaviour toward our genders can appear baffling but it is totally natural, and I have learned to tolerate it without any spite toward her or my brother. They are, after all, just a little bit insane.

My grandmother's first husband was short, The second was tall. One had a moustache and black wavy hair, the other did not. She has pictures of both husbands on either side of her bedroom wall where they hang quietly in the ordered little world that my grandmother has created inside her modest house for the last thirty years. She dusts the pictures daily with a handkerchief she keeps folded by her night table. The handkerchief is only for the photographs of the two men that hang on her wall. The third man hanging on a cross over the headboard of her bed she dusts with a feather brush.

The tall one's photograph is on the right. He was my grandfather and I can see something of me in the tranquil look of his young face with his receding hairline and large brow. His slightly crooked eyes with the droopy eyebrows are unmistakably similar to mine. He was gone five years before I came along, but when I look at the photo he does not appear to be a stranger, perhaps because I have spent so many years in this room, we have come to know each other. Sometimes when I am in my grandmother's room and we are chatting while I help her with some totally irrelevant chore like folding nightgowns and sheets or ironing pillowcases, I become as inquisitive with her as she is with me.

"*Nonna, tell me something, why did you marry these two men?*"

There is always a long dramatic pause before she attempts to find words to give me an answer. She could have been an actress. She prepares her stout little body to stand firm and proud as she clears her throat and places her fingers through her Anna Magnani mane, still thick and well-coloured. After a couple of deep sighs, she reminds me how very striking she was in her youth and how the suitors would not leave her alone. She had many to choose from as she recalls. There were plenty of handsome young men in that small southern town by the Adriatic who would have begged for her hand in marriage.

"I was too beautiful not to marry, so many want to make me their wife, so many, but I choose my first husband because that one he loves me."

Her cheeks darken with a blush as she turns to look at the picture of the man with the moustache. If the first one had not died, she would have been a fine lady in a fine house. If the first one had not died, she would have lived a pampered life. The first one was from a family of merchants, well established in local commerce and highly respected in their village, and she would have inherited much property in due time. But he died before he could give her children and without children there was little claim to position or property.

"In my time the women ... we marry ... we make children ... we become good wife, good mother, that's what we do."

There is a look in her eyes that is unconvincing, faintly distant, as if she might be trying to talk herself into believing her own words. Perhaps she is hoping that I will accept them without question. I believe she married the first one for love, the second she married because the first one died. He was not a man of business, came from a humble family of farmers, but he was the one who loved her completely. His family resented him for marrying a widow and did not attend the wedding, she tells me. It was the second who gave her the children and made me possible.

"A young widow no good in my days. For the womens in that time with no husband, you got nothing in the life, so you find the husband and you make the life."

The second one brought her to Toronto, to a house that was less than fine. It's the same house where the photographs now hang, where my mother was born, and where I played as a child among the knick-knacks and photographs. It is the same house where my grandmother waits for my drop-ins, where we sit on her bed and flip through memories in between folding laundry or making pots of espresso, which we drink as if we never had need to sleep again.

It is this house she will leave to my brother and me when her time comes, her simple and unpretentious legacy — her gift to us. She will leave us this house so we will remember, on occasion, that she once existed. Along with the house she will leave us the photographs and the bank account with her savings. She shows me where she keeps her bank book, in a special place, so I will know where to find it, when it's time.

But I do not know what house I will live in, or whom I will share it with. I don't know what I will remember if I live to be her age or if I will ever have children of my own. I cannot tell my grandmother my dreams because I know they would upset her. There are truths and desires in my life that have no words she will understand. I am as much a casualty of my time as she was of hers. Perhaps casualty is the wrong word. She was a product of her time, and chose what women were offered: men, marriage and God.

Do I tell her that a man is not what I want? Rather, marriage to a man is not what I want. My time, this place, allows me that choice. How do I make her understand that the world has changed? She sometimes looks on change as a kind of loss and at the same time states the opposite.

"*Nothing in the life change, people still people, bella mia.*"

In this room with her photographs and memories I choose

to remain the granddaughter who cannot find a man to make her a wife. While we fold sheets and iron pillowcases and talk of her lovers who hang dust free on pale blue walls, I choose to let her deny the passing of time. I know she can feel in her old, settled heart how much I love her. Some things between us will remain unspoken, no need for confession, but I know she understands. There is something between us that needs no words to be clear. She knows I am searching for so much more than a man, or even two, to "*make the life.*"

✤ GRAZIA ON GRACE ✤

Tiresome heart, forever living and dying,
House without air, I leave you and lock your door.
—Edna St. Vincent Millay, "Wild Swans"

CHRIST MAY HAVE STOPPED AT EBOLI but he never quite made it to Matera until Hollywood called. Matera is a town in the region of Basilicata somewhere around the calf of Italy's boot. It was the town coveted by a rich Hollywood star and destined to become the set for his film where he would explore the Passion of Christ. The Hollywood star turned director spent several years among the breathtaking ruins of the ancient town appraising the canvas where he would eventually record his celluloid masterpiece. It was in this town of primitive stone and rock, years before the Hollywood star had conceived of staging the biography of Jesus among its primal beauty, that Grazia received her marriage proposal, by mail.

Grazia Orsini was twenty-nine and already considered well past her prime to become a bride to an eligible suitor. Therefore her family had set in motion a well-planned search for a suitable candidate to become her husband. The search extended further than the stony confines of Matera and after months of communication through friends and relatives, they had been successful in securing the interest of a young gentleman who lived abroad, precisely in Canada (the other America), and it was from this interested and single gentleman that Grazia received her proposal.

The white envelope with the red and blue stripes at the edges had her name and address neatly written with a pen. The stamp with the image of the Queen of England precisely glued on the top right-hand corner of the envelope was almost spotless. Grazia held it in her hand, staring, and not quite sure if she should open the envelope or continue caressing it. She was well aware of her looming thirtieth birthday, time having become an adversary, so any proposal would have been something to contemplate, and she hoped this envelope would be her passport to fortune. She gently pulled apart the glued edges of the envelope and pulled out the folded white paper. As she read the neatly written words her face became soft and luminous, and the lids of her eyes closed in a moment of pleasure.

It was no surprise that she accepted the offer in the envelope without a flicker of hesitation but rather with an anticipation that left her curiously delighted.

Along with the concise offer of matrimony, well written in a cursive style that seemed to have been carefully manipulated, there was also a small black and white photograph of the interested suitor. The photo, from the waist up, showed a handsome stalwart face, a notably elegant head with dark hair that rested on two very broad shoulders. And although the lips on the prominent face were not full, they were sensuous and wide below a straight pleasing nose. The eyes were the right distance apart and appeared light in colour. Grazia was immediately impressed. You could say she was even a little excited at the good fortune that had fallen upon her. The image in the photograph projected a style and sophistication that she hoped would also exist in the man she would eventually meet.

Grazia slipped the photograph of her husband-to-be between her blouse and her breast where it would remain for several weeks (removed and placed on the dresser only at bedtime). The preparations for her eventual journey would take some months but she began packing the one large suitcase with her allotted dowry: a set of sheets, four linen towels, two monogrammed nightgowns, a lace trimmed tablecloth she had embroidered herself, and a wedding dress that had been passed on to her by her older married sister. Her second pair of shoes with slight heels, her gold earrings, and gold crucifix were her only luxuries.

The month of October was unusually warm that year and she was happy when the day came to travel to Naples, where she would board a ship for the long passage over the Atlantic to Halifax, Nova Scotia. She had never been anywhere farther than the city of Bari. She had only ever travelled on a train and a bus, and only once or twice in her life. She was jubilant at the thought of her adventure and more than happy to leave the antiquated ruins of Matera, those ruins that the Hollywood actor would find enchanting so many years later.

Grazia had never seen the beauty the Hollywood actor had found in his search for the hometown of Jesus. She had only ever felt the discomfort, the coldness of stone, the indifference of history, the poverty, and the impossibility of dreams. Grazia had dreams; they were uncomplicated, simple: a man of her own, children of her own, a home of her own, one that did not smell of rotting centuries and whose walls were not made of damp rock. Matera would never be the place of her dreams. Grazia welcomed the challenge, willing to go far to find her space, and unlike others before her who had left weeping and sad, broken-hearted and afraid, she was leaving with a smile as large as her face.

The port of Naples bustling with sounds and smells that invaded her senses made Grazia dizzy with pleasure. The enormous ship docked in the port was magnificent. There, on the head of the ship in bold black letters, was its name: Vulcania. What a magnificent name, she thought. Vulcania! It would be a wonderful name for a girl child one day.

Grazia was immersed in the noise and excitement around her. So many other young women with slightly lost and troubled eyes were also passengers. They seemed less assured in their situation as they crowded on the deck. So many young faces with already the etchings of fear, of confusion, and the pain of leaving behind all that they knew. The ship began to move. Grazia lifted her head to a cloud of white handkerchiefs all waving high in the air. The Vulcania slowly gliding into the open sea, a giant toy, sliding into waves and feathery clouds. She, too, waving her cotton handkerchief high above her head until the port of Naples no longer filled her eyes.

Twelve days to cross the ocean, twelve endless days and the sea was not pleasant. The waves were powerful, the rocking, the rolling, and hundreds of bellies inside out before the ship reached the shores of Nova Scotia. Before the two-day train ride to Union Station in Toronto and then to the house on Grace Street.

The photograph had not lied. The man was handsome and tall. Indeed his eyes were green, unusual for a man who came from a southern town high on the hilltops of Calabria, but it did not displease her. The man's smile was full of white teeth and yes, the hair was thick and clean. Tired as she was from the long passage, she had arrived safe and whole and filled with trust that she had made the right decision. Here it would all begin, it would be new.

As she stared into the green eyes of the tall man her heart fluttered a little at the thought of becoming a bride. The twelve nights spent on the tiny cot in the ship, Grazia had imagined herself beside this man. She had imagined being at the altar in the gown once worn by her sister, already once blessed. She hoped it would bring her luck. She envisioned the children she would have with the man in the photograph and what they would look like. If she would give birth to a girl she would name her Vulcania in honour of the vessel that brought her to this man. Her children would be special, fathered by such a fine man. She wanted as many children as fingers on her hand. Three boys and two girls, she thought. Two girls would be good insurance for her and the tall green-eyed man in their old age. Girls would stay close to home, she thought.

The house on Grace Street was big and solid. The groom to be had made sure Grazia would find in it the necessary things a new bride would expect. She would cook on a gas stove, turn on electric lights, and sleep in a bed with a real mattress made with coiled springs and wool, not one that had been stuffed with dried corn husks and horse hair. She would have running water that did not have to be fetched at a well but flowed cold and plentiful from a faucet into a sink. And even though the second floor flat was rented to a young family with a new baby, he assured her they would be very comfortable with the first floor and the basement (which was large and dry and perfect for storage). The house on Grace Street was a castle in contrast to the unforgiving volcanic rock structures of Matera where she had lived on the side of a mountain without any comforts. The house on Grace Street was warm, brightly lit, and Grazia was more than pleased, she was happy. But it was the green eyes on the tall, elegant man that lacked the spark of contentedness as he gazed on his promised bride. He seemed surprised in a quiet yet puzzled way as he stared at her without blinking, as if he was finding it a little difficult to breathe.

Grazia had come with a meagre dowry, but that was not a problem because he was not a greedy man. It had never been the dowry that had interested him, having made enough money of his own in the new country to be a free and successful man. Something about Grazia had taken him by surprise when he saw her. It was she who did not match the image on the photograph she had sent him in return. Her likeness had not shown the missing tooth in the corner of her smile or the pallid, bloodless complexion of her skin. The long braid of dark hair was gone. Her Lollobrigida curls were tight and dark and pasted to her skull, the unfortunate result of a permanent obtained at the town's beauty parlour the week before she left, in preparation. He noticed also when she had walked toward him that she had a slight, feeble limp. A long trip, a tired leg he had assumed, but later he learned it was the consequence of one leg being slightly shorter than the other. He had gazed down at her feet observing the heel of her right shoe; it appeared thicker and stood an inch or so taller than the left one. When she offered her hand across the table he had noticed the bony shape of her fingers, the roughness of her skin. Her flesh didn't lie. She had been much more intimate with a spade or a shovel, perhaps a pitchfork, than she had with a needle and thread or other more feminine tools. There was more of Matera in her than even Grazia had realized.

They sat facing each other at the kitchen table. The silence was awkward until she boldly asked him for a drink and he, embarrassed by his lack of welcome, promptly brought a bottle to the table, opened a kitchen cupboard and retrieved two glasses with long, thin stems. He then poured the red wine into the etched glass goblets and handed one to her. Grazia took the glass. Together they raised them in a gesture of good fortune and then they drank to each other.

It had been a long trip from her town of prehistoric rock to the house on Grace Street. To the man in the photograph who had paid for her ticket. She was determined to stay. Grazia was determined to wear her sister's wedding dress, unyielding and secure that she would assemble their marriage bed with the sheets in her dowry that had travelled with her. She was resolute that she would give birth to five children in the bed she would make with those sheets. She had come so far, alone, over an endless ocean with a photograph in an envelope tucked between her heart and her breast. She was not going back to the town of stone she had left behind.

Grazia stood up, put the wine glass down on the kitchen table and moved toward the tall elegant man. She held out her fingers and reached out to take his hands in hers. They were strong and huge, the hands of a working man but they were also warm, yielding and welcoming, as if they understood they now belonged there, entangled with hers.

His light, faraway eyes would never attain the glow that Grazia felt in the burning beneath her eyelids when she looked at him. His eyes were simply kind, calm, composed. But she did see in them the serene approval of her presence. And she was certain that what she also saw in them was a commitment and a promise the tall elegant man would honour for a lifetime.

BLONDE FOREVER

Come out of your closet. It's dark in there.
—Lawrence Ferlinghetti, "Challenges to Young Poets"

CHERYL TIEG'S FLAWLESS, FRESH FACE of the 1970s, sprinkled with freckles and lit by her alluring blue eyes, is still on a poster that hangs in the front window of Vicky's Hair Boutique on Dufferin Street south of Lawrence Avenue. In June of 1975, Vicky opened her very own hair salon (or "boutique" as she preferred to call it) and the very day the doors opened to her brand new boutique, Vicky proudly placed the three-foot poster of Cheryl in the front window where she has remained a faithful resident to this day. Cheryl Tiegs was the blonde supermodel on every magazine cover from *Cosmopolitan* to *Time* to *Vogue* to *Sports Illustrated* and any and all magazines that were published in that amazing decade, except perhaps for *The Catholic Register.* It was at the height of Cheryl's photographic reign that Vicky decided she would become a businesswoman and Cheryl would serve as Vicky's good luck charm.

The word "boutique" was popular in the seventies. So was the dream of running your own successful business in the hope of becoming financially independent and secure. If you dared to dream a little more ambitiously, then you could even aspire to becoming rich. Yes, the American dream was big in the seventies, even if you lived in Canada. Of course, it was more difficult to achieve the dream if you were a woman and almost impossible if you were an immigrant woman. In the seventies, women were less likely to be encouraged in their independence, and if they were in any way successful it was usually because their success was tied to their image as beautiful, desirable, and decorative creatures with perfect shapes (preferably hourglass), perfect hair (preferably blonde), perfect eyes (preferably blue), and a splash of sexy freckles. But times were changing.

Vicky was a woman without freckles and the camera had no particular fondness for her pretty but ordinary face, even if her eyes were blue. There were no magazines calling to offer a layout on their glossy pages and even if she might have nurtured the desire of being just like Cheryl Tiegs, she never once admitted it to anyone. Vicky knew she was smart, open-minded, and a hard worker. She had faith in herself, even if the times and the magazines didn't reflect her very ordinary world. She adored the models on the cover pages on the drug store shelves, but she was far more intrigued by the women who were appearing more frequently on radio talk shows, magazine articles, and television interviews speaking about the changing roles of women in society, about the struggle for recognition, equality, and liberation. Vicky was curious and liked to think of herself as a modern woman doing her part to change the direction of society. She wanted to be an active part of this new and modern world. This movement known as Women's Liberation was something she could connect with because in her heart she felt she was a feminist, if that was at all possible considering her cultural background and her strict Catholic upbringing, which allowed little room for anything resembling a struggle for equality.

Victoria Luisa Gambacorta was the youngest of four daughters, born to an immigrant Italian family who had settled in the west-end neighbourhood known as Kensington Market in 1965, when Vicky was twelve. Her father was the patriarchal head of the family (and as strict as he was he had a weakness for his daughters whom he adored) and his word was law. In Vicky's world, women had clear defined roles that they embraced without question. Her father, who had learned his trade as a butcher in Italy, had opened a meat shop with the financial help of his older brother who had sponsored him to Canada. He had named the meat shop after his hometown of Benevento. Benevento Meats was half way down Baldwin Street, west of Spadina Avenue. The upstairs apartment with two bedrooms, kitchen, bathroom and living room housed the family of six.

Vicky's mother had married when she was only eighteen and had no special skills, but she was strong, determined, and she worked side by side with her husband in the meat shop, making sure it was always spotless and orderly. Vicky and her sisters all attended school, but all of them helped out when they could. Each day after school the girls would come to the meat shop and learn how to slice the cold meats. They helped package and wrap the chicken legs and thighs and learned how to grind slabs of pork to stuff into sausages. Because she was the youngest, Vicky's job consisted mostly of wiping and sweeping and placing purchases into paper bags for customers. It was not a job she enjoyed much, although she did like meeting people and had a natural charm that made customers feel welcome. Vicky's father made sure the girls were rewarded with two dollars each at the end of every week.

Vicky's parents had no idea about feminism and the Women's Liberation movement. Nor did they have any real idea about the American dream, or about boutiques or about women like Cheryl Tiegs. They were simply hard-working immigrant parents who wanted to create a good life for themselves and their children, and they lived by their traditions and religious beliefs. But Victoria, who wanted to be called Vicky, had begun to dream a different dream when her father brought home that first television set as a Christmas gift for the family.

Vicky's father had managed to save enough money to indulge in a small luxury and surprised the family by bringing home a twenty-eight inch, black and white television their first Christmas in Canada. Vicky was hooked. The television became a new altar in the living room. It was positioned just beneath the large print of the Sacred Heart of Jesus by the bay window that looked down on Baldwin Street. Vicky's mother had draped a white lace embroidered fabric over the top and placed a miniature replica of the Vatican she had bought on a trip to Rome during her honeymoon. That black and white television instantly took hold of Vicky's imagination. It became her escape and she spent every spare moment she had sitting inches away from the screen, transfixed by its magic. Vicky was completely captivated with the new world she discovered through the glass screen. That little box took her out of Kensington Market, out of the meat shop, and into the black and white lives and worlds of so many different people. She envied the beautiful women on the television set who lived in foreign cities and wore fashionable clothes. She loved their elaborate hairstyles, their smart haircuts, and their perfectly elegant curls.

She was intrigued by these women who always fell in love with handsome and heroic men. Vicky became convinced that life could offer her more than a meat shop in Kensington Market. There were days when she lied to her parents about too much homework and missed going to help in the meat shop so she could hurry home after school where she would sit, alone, and watch whatever appeared on that charmed screen. It didn't really matter what program was on, whatever program it was, it was far away from Kensington Market and from the smell of butchered chicken and beef. She was tired of sweeping up sawdust, scrubbing the fatty counters, and she was tired of handling slabs of meat.

When Vicky entered St. Joseph Commercial High School she no longer regularly helped out at Benevento Meats. High school presented Vicky with a new excuse and a new escape from Benevento Meats. Her parents had always been supportive of their daughters' getting a good education and encouraged them to follow their dreams. But the very first day Vicky entered the Catholic girls high school, dressed in her wool uniform and black oxford shoes, she had a feeling she had made a mistake. The uniform itched and the shoes were unusually ugly. It was a small school, less than three hundred girls, all in blue wool dresses and unpleasant shoes. This was the school she had been advised to attend by her elementary school principal.

St. Joseph's Commercial turned out secretaries and receptionists with good typing, bookkeeping, and shorthand skills. Vicky had no interest in typing, or Pitman shorthand, but she was a quick learner and in the first six months at St. Joseph's she had mastered both. By the end of her first year in high school, she was typing sixty words a minute and was a natural with accounts receivable in bookkeeping. Vicky had also become popular with her classmates who had voted her as class Prefect. It was surprising that all this did not impress Sister Sebastian, her teacher, who was always reminding her that girls like her had limited choices in life. Sister Sebastian, in an orderly Catholic fashion, was preparing the girls to embrace, and excel in, their traditional role in society. But this was not what Vicky wanted. Once, when Vicky expressed the desire that she may want to go to college or university one day and possibly even start a business of her own after graduation, Sister Sebastian immediately put an end to Vicky's preposterous thoughts with her tactless remarks.

"That is absurd, absolutely absurd. You see Victoria, I have been teaching girls like you for a very long time and you will never make it. Girls like you should find a good husband and become good mothers. Girls like you should find work as secretaries or receptionists or perhaps a bank teller. That should be your aim in life."

As Vicky walked to the bus stop after school that day, she could not get Sister Sebastian's words out of her head.

"Girls like me? Girls like me?"

After her third year at St. Joseph's Commercial High School, Vicky left with her diploma and her commercial certificate that stated she could type 72 words a minute and she could take dictation of 112 words a minute in Pitman shorthand.

That next September Vicky enrolled in the Marvel School of Hairdressing.

*

Right next to the poster of Cheryl Tiegs hangs another famous blonde, equally beautiful but minus the freckles. Farrah Fawcett sparkles in the poster that had caused a lot of controversy back when Farrah was Charlie's sexiest angel because beneath that unbelievable blonde mane were two very perky breasts whose nipples stood firm and strong underneath a revealing bathing suit. Vicky too was blonde. Unusual for an Italian girl but Vicky's heritage was less southern than most of the immigrants from Italy and she had a maternal grandmother who had been adopted as a child and whose ancestry was somewhat of a mystery, although it was known she had been born in Lombardia. Vicky inherited her grandmother's blue eyes and blonde hair, but now the colour of her long straight seventies coiffure changes shade every three weeks or so, as does the tint of most of the customers she has served over the decades. Those customers who still have enough hair to colour come regularly.

The strip mall on Dufferin Street just north of Eglinton, where Vicky's boutique is located, has not changed much over the decades. The same squat, ugly buildings, with parking in front that have been there since the seventies and still stand today. It's a sad part of town with little to offer unless you have a particular reason to venture out that way. There are plenty of car dealerships or repair shops that line the long street. On grey wintery days, it is a wasteland. Vicky's boutique is smack in the middle of Wong's Convenience and Home Hardware. Just a few doors away is the Tim Horton's where Vicky stops every morning, except Sunday and Monday when the boutique is closed, for her usual double-double and blueberry muffin.

There had been hope for Dufferin Street in the seventies. New immigrants to the city offered possibilities of growth and change to the area, but it never truly became desirable. On Sunday afternoons, she and her friends would go dancing at the Piper Club on the East side of Dufferin. The garage-like structure was dark and cavernous, but brimming with young immigrant girls whose traditional parents would only allow them to socialize on Sunday afternoons, and who were expected to be home before the sun went down. It was also full of young immigrant boys. Those Sunday afternoon dances were one of the few ways available to young immigrant women of that time to meet young immigrant men. This would not have fared well with the new women's liberation movement that Vicky wanted to be a part of, but on Sunday afternoons she too wanted some fun and she joined her friends and her sisters as they all headed for the Piper Club in anticipation of a romantic encounter with a handsome young man. Dufferin Street was home to a couple of dance halls that catered to the young immigrants on Sunday afternoons. The Rotonda, built in the shape of the Coliseum with arches that proudly announced "we're Italian," seemed grand in those days. Oh, those afternoons with live local bands, playing all the latest Italian pop tunes. Dozens of handsome Italian boys would come dressed in their hippest outfits, smoking cigarettes and driving cute little Fiats. It was a challenge to be romantic in those little cars. Avoiding the stick shift and finding a comfortable spot in those tiny seats, while wearing the obligatory girdles Vicky's generation was cursed with, could be awkward to say the least. But it didn't stop anyone from discovering romance in all those cool Fiats and sporty Camaros that crammed the parking lot behind the Piper Club. It was at one of those dances that Vicky met the handsome Gerardo, who called himself Jerry, and who drove a shiny red Mustang.

If Dufferin Street had promised possibilities in those early years, they never quite materialized. The Piper Club was gone by the eighties and the Rotunda became a church for evangelists.

More and more people of Vicky's generation seemed to head out to newer spaces, large subdivisions to the north of the city. Vicky was a city girl and had no desire to move north. She decided she enjoyed serving her customers exactly where she was on that non-inspiring street called Dufferin. She bought the plain little two-storey building in the strip mall and put her name on a large purple sign, *Vicky's Hair Boutique.* Then she placed Cheryl and Farrah in the front window and it was business as usual.

*

In the 1970s Vicky's blonde, straight, flowing hair was something to envy. Girls all wanted hair like Vicky's. Girls wanted to be Cheryl and Farrah and Vicky made them believe they could be. But the girls of today have no interest in blonde hair, freckles, and fluid locks of Vicky's generation and neither are they interested in a boutique in a strip mall on Dufferin Street, preferring the fancy spas and salons of a sophisticated and modern downtown Toronto.

Vicky has learned to be content with the thinning hair on the heads of faithful old customers and the occasional walk-ins. The women of her mother's generation still come for their monthly colour and cut, and tip her the same two dollars they tipped twenty years ago. The new residents in the neighbourhood, whose long braids are often covered by lovely scarves, seem reluctant to come into her shop although on occasion Vicky is challenged by the requests of a new customer who will bare her head to reveal black torrents of lustrous hair.

If Vicky has ever entertained the thought of closing up shop, she has erased it as quickly as it has entered her brain. Without Vicky's Hair Boutique she would simply be Victoria

Gambacorta, wife to Gerardo (Jerry) Martelli, mother to Alfie and Gloria, sister of Gina, Adele, and Livia, daughter of Ginevra and Rosario Gambacorta, the retired butcher. But every morning, when Vicky picks up her double-double and blueberry muffin and walks into her boutique, she turns on the radio and she forgets about Victoria and girls like her. Victoria is one of those girls Sister Sebastian tolerated all those years ago. Vicky is someone else.

Vicky's Hair Boutique is in a strip mall between a convenience store and a hardware store on an ordinary Toronto street that has never really evolved. It is not the American dream one would aspire to and even less a Canadian one. But it is where Vicky knows who she is. It is where she goes each day and finds not only herself, but Cheryl and Farrah waiting for her, content, and blonde forever.

ANNA AT THE WINDOW

Sometimes she gets
tired.
She has to carry
all this stuff around. It's not a
lot. It's a lot of small pieces, pieces.

—Rose Romano, "This Is Real"

ANNA PULLED ASIDE THE HEAVY BROCADE drapes of her living room window at exactly seven-thirty each morning and looked out to check what the weather was like. The front window on the second floor flat above the sushi restaurant, that had once been a grocery store, looked onto the north side of College Street. If the weather was good, Anna would walk down the stairs and unlock the two serious safety locks of the front door and step out onto the sidewalk. Rarely did the weather alter her routine except for the days when ice layered the sidewalk. In her flat black shoes, her moss green wool jacket with the multicoloured scarf around her neck, and her small leather purse over her arm, she walked with careful steps along the south side of College Street, past Clinton Street and toward Grace Street.

She regularly timed her stroll as she headed to St. Francis of Assisi Church for morning mass. It took her about twelve minutes if she did not stop to speak to anyone, otherwise it could take her twenty minutes or more if she was at all distracted or interrupted. It seemed that each year, as she added birthdays, she also added minutes to her walk. She did not blame her age for the extra time it took her to reach her destination. She simply liked walking slower now because there was no reason to hurry.

"Jesus will not mind," she would reassure herself. "He will be there even if I am late."

Anna was aware that the parish priest, Father Bastiano, was often late himself some mornings, giving in to the venial sin of an extra ten minutes sleep as his birthdays also accumulated.

Anna had noticed how fewer and fewer people in the neighbourhood attended the Italian mass. She was concerned that God and religion had become old and unnecessary for this new generation, as old and unnecessary as she sometimes felt. She rarely saw any young people sitting in the pews during mass, and if there were a few, it seemed they were only there to accompany their elders. The usual bodies were a handful of widows and widowers, and those who were tied to faith by tradition, loneliness, and perhaps a little fear. They gathered in the first three or four pews closest to the altar each morning and greeted each other with cordial handshakes, then sat quietly in the dimness of the empty space around them, waiting for the entrance of Father Bastiano and for the ceremony to begin. They never complained when Father Bastiano was late. If priests were allowed to retire then Father Bastiano was well past his expiry date, but slow moving and partially deaf as he was, he was still the Franciscan in charge and deserving of their respect and gratitude, which he received in abundance and with loyalty.

Anna had always felt safe and protected inside the walls of St. Francis of Assisi Church. It was the one place that seemed to have diverted the inevitable changes that had come to her neighbourhood and, for Anna, it was a place she understood. It had, for the moment, escaped the gutting and re-structuring that had been the fate of many of the old Victorian and Eduardian buildings on the surrounding streets. It was the one free-standing and beautiful hundred-year-old structure that had escaped the forces of change, holding onto its history.

As gentrified as her neighbourhood had now become, the church seemed to have gone unnoticed. It comforted her to know that it was still there; that she could walk to its doors, when they were unlocked, and enter without any reservation. Anna felt safe beneath its roof, surrounded by stained glass windows and statues of angels and saints, although she missed the smell of wax candles burning. They had been replaced by small electric lights in the shape of candles. This was the church's only modern addition and the reason for the change may have been the fear of a fire starting from lit candles. Anna wasn't exactly sure why they had replaced the wax candles with electric ones, but she paid her three dollars each time and pushed the minute button that switched on the electric flame that illuminated the red glass container beneath the statues of the saints. She lit one for St. Anthony each morning after mass. The Saint of lost things. She prayed for her church to be there long after she was gone.

For more than fifty years, Anna had accumulated memories within the walls of St. Francis. She remembered the very early days, back in the sixties, when all the Italian immigrants would attend the church of St. Agnes at the corner of Dundas and Grace Street. But that had long ago become the church the Portuguese community favoured. St. Francis was her church, where she was always welcomed by a thirty-foot figure of the Ascending Jesus in white robes just above the altar. She had walked down the church's long aisle to her about-to-be husband, Oreste, and taken her marriage vows beneath that Jesus. It was the church where old Father Germinio, who had died years ago, had baptized her only son and later given him first communion and confirmation. It comforted her to think that this would also be the church where her funeral will take place, when the time comes.

Anna and Oreste had married in their twenties. Young and very much in love, they moved into a two-room flat on the third floor of Mrs. Santacroce's house on Euclid Avenue. The two-room flat with a bed, a few chairs, a small kitchen table, and an assortment of utensils suited them just fine. Mrs. Santacroce's house was a safe, temporary shelter for many new couples beginning their lives together. It was also a sanctuary for many lonely immigrant boarders whose families had been left behind in the old country. It was a large, bright house, always bustling with people. Mrs. Santacroce, a tiny round woman, sixty inches tall, with a bellowing but warm voice, and hair that challenged any brush to unravel her curls, loved the noise and commotion. She enjoyed the guests in her home and welcomed the dollars she stashed away from the rents. She also earned extra dollars cooking and cleaning for her boarders who had no wives. Mrs. Santacroce was very clever and had a good head for business. Eventually she bought two more homes on Euclid Avenue and continued her success as a landlord until her death in 1989.

A few weeks after they had settled into their new flat, Anna found work in Luis Staub's shirt factory, located by Spadina and Adelaide. The factory was a good half hour walk from Euclid Street and Anna often skipped the streetcar ride and walked all the way. She worked an eight-hour shift, until five p.m. from Monday to Friday, and on her return home she indulged in the streetcar ride only when her legs felt heavy and painful from standing for too many hours on an unyielding concrete floor.

Anna had a natural talent with a needle and thread, and Mr. Staub recognized quickly what an asset she would become to his business, giving her plenty of overtime work anytime she wanted a little extra cash. Her quick fingers and fine eye for detail in stitching were gifts that had been exercised as a child with her grandmother's attention and teaching. She was good with patterns and scissors, and often Mr. Staub had her cutting and designing alongside him. She soon earned not only the trust, but the admiration of both her boss and her co-workers.

Oreste had been apprenticed as a baker in his youth and he found work with the Beaver Bread Company in Toronto, which was just off Dufferin Street. There he made fresh loaves of white, soft, English bread and sweet sugary doughnuts, as well as thick pizza with tomato sauce that was packaged and delivered to homes and shops. The doughnuts and white bread were not what he was accustomed to baking, but he quickly mastered the art of these new products. One day he would open his own bakery and return to the recipes he had safely tucked in his notebooks and memory. The Beaver Bread Company allowed Oreste a decent wage and the opportunity to work at what he loved. In three short years, the diligent couple had saved enough money for a down-payment on their own property and said goodbye to Mrs. Santacroce's third floor flat. Mrs. Santacroce, not one to waste time or money, already had another couple moving in the very day Anna and Oreste were leaving.

Anna had wanted a house with a garden but Oreste had convinced her that a commercial property where he could one day open his own business would be a better deal. So they put four thousand dollars down on a three-storey building on the south side of College Street that Anna still calls home.

In 1962, their only son, Saro, was born and by the time he went to school Anna and Oreste had paid off the mortgage on their building. Paying off the mortgage was almost a sacred event and a serious priority in their lives. They saved every penny, every nickel in those early years. Work, church, family, and a few friends were the only things Anna had known most of her life.

"So many prayers since then," she would often repeat to herself on her way to church. Sometimes she would stop to speak to the few recognizable faces that remained in the neighbourhood. She enjoyed exchanging greetings and an occasional anecdote of a shared past, the good and the bad times, with anyone who had a few minutes to spare.

At seven-thirty in the morning the neighbourhood was still recognizable. At that time of day, the street was easier to navigate and she felt she still belonged among the clatter of ordinary things: delivery trucks, streetcars, people on their way to work, regular folk and their routines. At seven-thirty in the morning there were fewer bodies to plot a course through, and the neighbourhood still felt like home even if the changes were more than Anna was able to embrace. But life now was filled with change. The area now catered to a different crowd, a different way of life, and although she understood that time had moved and that was the natural way of the world, it did not make her feel any better. Time is about loss, she thought, and loss is never a good thing.

Everywhere along the north and south side of College, cafés, bars, and restaurants had replaced the shops and small businesses that once made the neighbourhood a unique part of the city. Now it was possible to drink a martini anytime of the day, but to buy an onion you had to make a pilgrimage five or six long blocks down to the Metro, where everything seemed to be wrapped in plastic, not very fresh and much too expensive.

She missed Mr. Wasserman's bakery that had stood so proudly on the corner of Grace Street, with its elegant yellow and black lettering on the glass window where he displayed the delicious bagels, the rye loaves, and the lovely Jewish pastry filled with cheese and jams. She missed the Black Sea Fish Market where she could look into the eyes of whole fish to see how fresh they were. If the eyes were clear and not cloudy, then she knew the fish was fresh and perfect. The fishmonger was a big Greek man with plump red cheeks who would always clean and scale the fish for her. She bought fish twice a week for Oreste, on Fridays and Wednesdays. On days when fish and pasta were not on the menu, Anna would go down the street to Beatrice Avenue where the Sicilian butcher, who was never without his striped cap and a bright red apron, greeted her by tipping his hat. With a raspy, tuneful voice he'd shout, "*Buon giorno, signora Anna, e buon appetito.*"

There she would buy rabbit and tripe for Oreste and Saro, and thick juicy pieces of veal shoulder for hearty broths and sauces. The butcher always threw in a couple of bones thick with marrow for flavouring, and he never charged her anything extra. The next stop was a short walk past Montrose Avenue to Trimonti Fruit Market where she would negotiate a better price for peppers and eggplants, and then spend time chatting with Mrs. Trimonti about all her children. She missed Mr. Morrison's fabric shop with its wonderful selection of linens. Anna would often choose an unusual fabric to sew an elegant dress that she would wear on special and festive occasions. Mr. Morrison, with his tape measure around his neck and his reading glasses halfway down his nose, always gave her a good price and sometimes, as a favour, she would do alterations for his customers in return.

Most of all Anna missed the tall and handsome gentleman who ran the Rosticceria e Caffé, and who spoke with a fine Italian accent. Each day he would roast the coffee beans in the big round machine he had in the window next to open canvas bags filled with different varieties of coffee beans from Mexico and South America. The aroma would escape each time the door opened to his shop. How Anna had loved the smell of that coffee. She would go in twice a week to buy a quarter pound of freshly roasted beans and treat herself to an espresso while she waited. She could have bought a pound all at once, but she enjoyed returning to the shop twice a week to savour the aroma and to listen to the lovely accent of the proprietor. The handsome gentleman whose name she now cannot recall was refined and polite and often did not charge her for the espresso she drank as she waited. When she left his shop, the tall gentleman always opened the door for her. Rarely did anyone open doors for her now, or tip their hats.

So much of the life she had known on College Street had disappeared. Those who were fortunate enough to remain, like her, were stubbornly tied to the street with a fierce loyalty. They could not be easily convinced to leave the homes they had worked tirelessly for, especially if they could still manage to take care of themselves and to reason clearly without assistance. They were a generation of survivors, not easily manipulated by forces outside, still in charge of their lives, and they greeted each other daily in church. But Anna was aware each time she sat in the pews of St. Francis that there were fewer and fewer survivors filling the first three rows in front of the altar.

*

Anna cherished the mornings. Rarely did she walk out of her second-floor flat when the sun went down. The neighbourhood changed when the sun went down. She liked to watch the transformation from the large window that in the evening framed everything under the street lights, her living room window, where she often sat gazing out at the street below. She looked forward to watching the street at night, which brought out strange behaviours in the people who favoured the dark. It was so different from the days when she was young, when they had to keep walking toward a destination, always respectful and aware of others. Those days they could not linger for long; everyone was made to feel a bit suspect, and police officers made sure there was no loitering about the neighbourhood. But now the crowds of mostly young people in search of entertainment linger without interference for hours on the street, in the cafés, in local night spots. They were often noisy and rowdy, especially on weekends, the music from the bars blaring late into the night as groups of people smoking cigarettes huddled together on the sidewalks. Anna sometimes thought she had lived too long, that there were too many changes to adjust to. But in some strange way, the changes also kept Anna aware that life still existed and yes, it was different, but it was life, and watching it from her window was better than watching television.

Her son Rosario, whom she called Saro, had pleaded with her to leave the old neighbourhood and to move closer to where he and his family were living, but she would not hear of it. For years he tried to coax her out of that flat, concerned for her safety and her comfort, all those stairs to climb. But Anna's knees were still strong and the stairs were not a problem.

Saro, her only son, had moved away with his young wife in the eighties, when the neighbourhood had begun to change. Saro had bought a big house with lots of rooms on a street that could not be reached by a streetcar. Anna only went to their house on special occasions, when Saro would pick her up in his van. Saro and his wife had several children who had grown up far from College Street, but now that they were grown and drove their own cars they often made their way downtown and to the clubs on College Street, but seldom did they climb the stairs to Anna's flat for a visit.

Anna's second floor flat was comfortable. The building belonged to her. Oreste had been a smart businessman. He had bought the building when the price was right, long before the craziness of the prices had driven so many away from the neighbourhood. The downstairs sushi restaurant and the third floor rented flat paid a good and reasonable rent and, along with her old age pension, Anna had her independence. She had no reason to worry about money and for that she was grateful. Oreste had provided well and she had been a careful, even frugal, woman and had saved the pennies when necessary. She had worked long hours next to her husband in the bakery he had opened after leaving the Beaver Bread Company where he had worked for fifteen years. And this would be after the sewing and mending and ironing that she did everyday, leaving her daily workplace to join Oreste in the bakery and do whatever needed to be done.

There was little time left in Anna's days for social activities but she had struck up a friendship with the widow Carbone who ran the local cheese and salami shop a few doors away. Virginia Carbone had been widowed young and left with two sons who were a little older than her Saro. Sometimes Anna found herself helping Virginia with the two boys, often having them over for supper when Virginia couldn't find the time to cook. The boys were polite young men and they became older brothers to her Saro. The two families shared many years together, watching the boys grow into fine young men. But Mrs. Carbone's health had not been kind to her and she was still a young woman when her sons had to place her in the rest home. The last time Anna had gone to visit her friend at the rest home, Virginia did not recognize her. Anna would not return to visit her again.

The flat seemed empty now that Oreste was gone, and Saro and Virginia's boys were grown and had gone on to live their lives. And since Virginia had been placed in a rest home, Anna had also lost her best friend. For thirty years, she and Oreste had been up at dawn and in bed at midnight, working every hour of the day, with only Sunday to look forward to when they could sleep an extra hour or two. Life had been hard, but it had been good. But all that was done now.

"We all end up alone sooner or later," she'd mumble to herself whenever she dusted the photo of Oreste in the silver frame. She had placed the photograph on the dining room table covered with a lace tablecloth that Anna had decorated with her fine needlework. The red thread of tiny poppies circled the edge of the fine lace all perfectly stitched into the delicate material. No one but she ate at the dining room table anymore and Anna made sure the photograph of Oreste was prominently placed beside a vase of fresh flowers or a large, perfumed candle. Sometimes, when she felt the urge, she would bake something sweet and leave a slice or a biscuit next to the silver frame for Oreste as she silently ate her dinner by his photo. Anna was proud of the tablecloth and the silver frame that showed Oreste's generous face with those lucid eyes, large and round, without the heavy lids of his later years. It was the face of the young man who had stolen her heart instantly on a New Year's Eve almost sixty years ago. They had been on their way to the church dance in the basement hall of St. Francis Church. The New Year's Eve dance was the event of the year for the new immigrants of Little Italy.

The church hall would fill with young folk, elders, children and babies, happy and excited to welcome the arrival of a new year. There would be food provided by the women, wine by the men who made it, and music by anyone who played an accordion or a guitar, and everyone would be dressed in their finest outfits. There would be laughter and dancing and storytelling and then without fail someone would start to sing an old familiar Italian tune that would bring everyone to tears.

Anna had noticed Oreste because he was so much taller than most of the other men in the room. Tall and striking, he wore a tie with elegance, as if he had worn one all his life, not uncomfortably like the other men who tugged at theirs, loosened them, and then left them hanging sloppily around their necks. Oreste wore his with a distinctive style that Anna found exciting. She found herself staring at him throughout the night. How impressed she was by his strong features and gentle face. He too had noticed the slight girl in the blue and white dress. He had watched her as she walked up to light a candle by the statue of Mary, an offering for a blessing of a good year to come. The candle must have worked because that evening Oreste introduced himself. Six months later they were married and a year later their only child, Saro, was born.

Saro had grown up to be a successful man and a good son. He made daily phone calls to his mother, always spoke with a polite and concerned tone, and he made sure Anna had everything she needed. Saro also took care of any repairs or jobs necessary in Anna's flat, but his was a busy life and it left him little more than the absolute necessary time for Anna. Saro's wife and his children lived a long way from College Street and their visits were rare. Anna made few demands on their time, and was grateful for Saro's phone calls and his visits on Sundays. But she missed her men and their needs. Anna missed their large presence, their loud energy that had once filled the flat with life. She missed taking care of someone.

Part 2

Angelina had always hated her name and had called herself Lina from the time she entered grade school in that little town near Lake Huron called Petrolia. Such a weird name for a town she thought. Why would anyone call a town Petrolia? Oh, she was aware it had to do with the oil plant and petrol. That was obvious. It was impossible to escape the smell of that town. The smell of oil was everywhere, in the soil, in the air, on the plants. But what a stupid name for a town, she thought. And what was her mother thinking naming her Angelina? It wasn't even her grandmother's name or anything like that, and Angelina Jolie wasn't around when she was born so it couldn't have been because her mother liked the actress. Angelina was simply a name her mother liked and so she got stuck with it. But it was better than Iona, which was the name her mother had been brutally branded with. Iona's Irish blood, mixed with Armando Pescatrice's southern Italian blood, had produced Angelina Rosina Pescatrice, a mouthful for anyone but, in the town of Petrolia, it was a mouthful and more. Angelina couldn't stand her name or her town so she became Lina and ran away from both her name and the town as soon as she could muster the courage and the dollars she needed to get to the big city. Lina was eighteen and Iona and Armando were reluctant to let her go but they could do nothing to stop her.

Lina hitched a ride to London, Ontario, on a transport truck that was headed east. She stopped in London for a few days, checked out the town a bit, slept at the bus station for a couple of nights. But London was a hick town, not very different from Petrolia, she thought, and it just wouldn't do. Lina was determined to make her way to the big city, Toronto, determined to get away from the strange names and the smallness of everything around her.

It wasn't that Lina's life was particularly messed up or unpleasant, it was simply because life where she lived seemed boring and small. Lina had finished high school, but high school had offered her little in terms of dreams or ambitions and even less skills that she could offer the world. And she wasn't about to mirror or repeat the dull life of her mother. Not that her mother's life was particularly unhappy, but to Lina it seemed uninteresting and lacklustre. Her mother was just a mother and a wife who kept a nice house and who worked at the local hardware store as a cashier and as a part-time accountant. Lina's father had married Lina's mother right after high school, and Lina was born a year later.

Armando Pescatrice, Lina's father, had always loved cars and he had worked for years at the local garage owned by old man Pappy Poruzzo, until one day when he had saved enough money to buy the garage from Pappy when Pappy retired. The garage does well and Lina's father has been running it for years, making a decent living for the family. Lina's parents seemed content in Petrolia with the hardware store, the garage, and their neat house by the lake, and they didn't seem to mind the smell that surrounded them on hot nights in summers. But Lina wanted a bigger life. Lina wanted a bigger city and off she went looking for it. That is how she landed on College Street.

*

It had begun as a light drizzle that quickly turned to rain the morning Anna walked by the Royal Cinema on her way to church. She hadn't thought of taking the umbrella and had been reluctant to climb back up all those stairs to fetch one. She stopped for a short while under the awning of the Royal Cinema waiting for the rain to weaken. That very morning Lina, who had found her way to the neighbourhood, had also taken refuge underneath the large theatre sign. She was a small bundle squatting on the cement with her duffle bag by her side and a tall coffee paper cup in her hand. Anna couldn't help but stare at the young girl, a little waif of a girl, like one of the young creatures she watched from her living room window at night when the sun went down. She wondered why the young girl was up so early, and sitting beneath a theatre marquis with a duffle bag and a coffee cup, while it poured. Neither one said a word to the other. The rain shrivelled to a dribble and Anna headed toward the church, leaving Lina to her solitude and her coffee cup.

It had been one of those spring days when the clouds moved slowly and the sky was slathered with a damp grey mist that promised nothing. On her way home, Anna noticed that the young girl was gone. She continued toward the flat thinking about what she would prepare for dinner. Tonight she would make a soup. Rainy days always seemed to inspire the making of a thick tasty soup. She had all the ingredients at home and had left the romano beans soaking in the pot before she had gone out. They would be ready to cook when she got home. Carrots, potatoes, celery, a sweet large onion, beans and tomatoes. Yes, she'd make a delicious, thick minestrone soup tonight, she thought.

That evening as she opened the window to look out on her neighbourhood she felt a gust of wind that had returned with a blustery temper. There were few people moving about on the street, which seemed unusual, and as she looked over at the lights of the Royal Cinema she could see someone huddled beneath the sign. The young girl had re-appeared under the bright blue and white lights, still avoiding the rain. Anna stared at the young girl for a while then shut the window and headed to the kitchen. Anna opened a few drawers and found the container she wanted. She scooped a couple of ladles of minestrone into the plastic container and covered it. Then, she grabbed a spoon, wrapped it in a napkin, and put it in a bag. She had always been reluctant to step out into the neighbourhood at night but tonight she didn't seem to feel any fear. Tonight she picked up the umbrella, put on her coat, went slowly down the stairs, unlocked the serious locks and walked towards the

Royal Cinema where Lina sat crosslegged on her duffle bag against the brick wall.

Anna stopped, looked down on the young girl, extended her arm and offered her the container of soup.

"I make this soup, very warm, you eat."

Lina's puzzled reaction was not a surprise. Who was this crazy lady, she thought? A few seconds passed before she spoke.

"Thanks, but, no, no, thank you very much, I ... I don't like soup, but thank you."

"Everybody like soup," Anna responded. "Soup is good. You try, it make you warm up, this weather very bad for getting sick, you try. You will like. I make myself."

Lina reached out a little reluctantly and accepted the container Anna handed to her.

"I make good soup, you will like it. Try, try."

Lina lifted the lid to the plastic container; the aroma was familiar and the warm container felt good in her cold hands.

"What is your name?" Anna asked.

Without thinking Lina responded, "Angelina."

"Angelina ... beautiful name. Angelina means little angel in my language," Anna offered.

"I know." Lina smiled as she brought a spoonful of soup to her mouth.

"Why you out here in the rain? You don't have a home to go there?" Anna asked with a concerned tone.

Lina felt uncomfortable with the old woman's curiosity and she simply shrugged her shoulders in a dismissive gesture.

"I am Anna, I live over there." Anna pointed to her building. "You see the window up there, I see you from the window."

"Thank you for the soup, it's very good." Lina continued to spoon the soup into her mouth without stopping.

"You welcome. You finish. I go home now. Maybe soon you go home too. Not good to be on the street, alone at night, in the rain, no good."

Lina watched as Anna made her way slowly to the front door of the building across the street. Anna turned to look at the young girl again and waved at her before she went in. The soup was good and Lina emptied the container and licked the spoon.

The next morning when Anna drew aside the drapes and looked out at the day the young girl was gone. For a moment Anna felt pleased, hoping the girl had found her way home where she belonged. When she went past the Royal Cinema on her way to church she saw the abandoned spoon and empty container. This morning she would say some extra prayers for Angelina.

That evening, after she had routinely eaten her meal sitting alone at the table by Oreste's photograph, Anna made her way to the window and lifted it halfway, just enough to keep her head from banging into it. She pulled the cushion from the couch and placed it on the ledge and leant her arms into it as she looked down on the street. The rhythm of the traffic had changed. The lights were flickering and the crowds beginning to move in varying speed in search of their favourite spots. Anna enjoyed this time of the evening. Yesterday's rain was a memory. The sun had been constant all day and as the spring warmed toward summer the evening light was beautiful, and watching the young people in their frenzied energy move about the neighbourhood brought a little excitement to her old eyes. Anna was content to watch and to listen as the world moved on. Sometimes she would pull up the chair and linger at the window until her eyelids argued the hour on the clock and she'd close the window and go to bed.

This particular spring night was mild and clear and even a star or two could be seen in the sky, which was rare because of all the city lights. The bulbs of the Royal Cinema were sputtering and Angelina was nowhere to be seen. Anna was glad the girl had found her way home. This night Anna sat a little longer in her chair by the window, folded her arms and listened to the music coming from the open doors of the College Street Bar. It was not the music that she had danced to in the church hall the night she met Oreste. There was no tango or waltz to move to in her head. It was not the music she enjoyed listening to on her favourite radio station in the afternoon, but she did not mind the persistent drumming and almost found herself tapping her foot to the loud, strange beat. This night she was not sleepy at all and her eyes were wide open. She sat and glimpsed the half moon that looked down on her and thought of Oreste and Saro and Virginia. Then she turned towards the Royal Cinema and thought about the young Angelina.

It was well after eight the next morning when Angelina appeared again under the Royal Cinema's awning, a tall Starbucks coffee cup in one hand and a muffin in the other. Angelina hoped she would see the old woman again today to thank her for her kindness and for that awesome soup. She looked up and down the street as she sipped from the tall cup, and then she turned her head toward the building that Anna had disappeared into on that rainy night. Angelina could see the window was open as the drapes moved lightly in the morning draft. If she had been closer to the building she might have seen a cushion slightly over the edge of the window frame. In the half-open window the head of a woman rested on her folded, still arms. Anna's serene and silent face fanned by the calm movements of her brocade drapes lay beautiful and quiet. College Street was almost awake.

TABLE FOR TWO

In the room the women come and go
Talking of Michelangelo.
—T. S. Eliot, "The Love Song of J. Alfred Prufrock"

RENZI, ROSSI AND SUTTON'S NINE-FOOT oak doors, exclusively designed by Pagani and Porzia of Woodbridge, shut early on Friday afternoons. Rita, the office manager/receptionist (who was always the last one in the office to leave), moved about fervently, locking up files and tidying up desks. As she tapped on the switch that lowered the blinds, she took a final look around before picking up her purse and keys. She couldn't help but glance at herself in the full-length baroque mirror by the door before making a quick exit. Her reaction was always the same. "God, I look tired."

Rita's weekend began at two p.m. and she couldn't bear to spend even an extra minute inside the offices of Renzi, Rossi and Sutton, who never came to the office at all on Fridays. As she turned the key in the lock she patted the triple lion head doorknob of pure brass and cheerfully said, "*arriverderci, boys.*"

Rita was two flights of stairs away from freedom on a Friday afternoon. Two flights of stairs away from anything that had to do with litigation, lawyers and real estate, and one bottomless sigh before she made her way down the buffed marble steps. Rita often avoided stepping into the elevator for fear an electrical malfunction might keep her prisoner in the building longer than she could stand. A steady, firm hand on the banister till she reached the ground floor and she would be free.

On Fridays Rita regularly met her friend Costanzia at the Market Lane Café, a short walk from the offices of Renzi, Rossi and Sutton. The women looked forward to a couple of hours of girl talk with cappuccino and pastry to plan their weekend before heading home. Rita and Costanzia were attractive, single women of a certain age who had managed to escape marriage in their younger years and who enjoyed their independence and freedom. Rita had just moved into a brand new apartment north of Highway 7 on Islington Avenue, which she shared with Stella, her cat. Costanzia, her friend, was an only child who lived with her parents in a sprawling estate in the country, just north of the town of Kleinburg. Costanzia, who had inherited her father's successful travel agency, and which she had turned into an even more successful business with her astute sense of investment, had met Rita on one of those all-inclusive vacations in Aruba many winters ago and they had become good friends. Costanzia loved to travel and lived a life with little worry since her father had provided her with a healthy financial portfolio and a solid inheritance in both cash and real estate. She could come and go whenever she pleased. Rita was less financially secure but had worked for Renzi, Rossi and Sutton for over twenty years, earning a good salary that she saved and invested carefully. Her pension and savings and mortgage-free condo would see her comfortably through her old age, considering she had no children or family to support. Rita's parents had moved back to their Italian village after their retirement, having expressed the desire to die in the land where they had been born. Rita found herself alone but not unhappy. Having only Stella the cat to take care of, her only worry was emptying the litter box.

Costanzia was always first to arrive at the café, less hindered by the time on the clock than Rita was, and being a creature of habit regularly chose the third table by the window. She was sometimes bold enough to ask a patron to move if they were occupying the table she wanted. She sat with her chair facing the parking lot keeping a loving eye on her new, orange Fiat 500, which stood out because of its brilliant colour. A number of Fiat 500s began appearing regularly in the parking lot at Market Lane. They were rapidly becoming the new trendy vehicle of choice, but they were in the more traditional colours and Costanzia's bright orange one, with the deep lilac interior, certainly could not go unnoticed.

When Rita arrived the cappuccino had already been ordered; she simply had to choose the pastry she preferred that day. Costanzia didn't indulge in pastry, but allowed herself an almond *biscotto* that she loved to dunk in her coffee. Rita never passed up the occasion for a sweet treat, especially on Fridays, and was particularly fond of the rum-drenched and custard-filled brioche. Today she would be extra indulgent and ask for whipped cream as an added delight. Today she had a colossal craving (which she always blamed on the full moon) for extra sugar.

*

Ciao, ciao, cara, give us a kiss. God I am tired. You would not believe the paperwork I had to organize and file today.

Computers my royal *culo,* the paperwork in the office is as bad as it ever was, if not worse. Hope the three wise men at their holy golf club appreciate my talents and my work. Fridays are really a pain.

Sit down, tired lady, take a load off those pinched toes. If they're at the golf club then they know they left their bank books in good hands; they appreciate you, no doubt. Want to hear how many flights my agents booked today?

Spare me unless they booked one for me.

I thought people were feeling an economic crisis. You'd never know it by their travel plans. Europe, Hawaii, Japan, Australia, standard vacation spots ... boggles the mind, but I'm not complaining, let them vacation ... ah, here's the coffee, finally.

Well, I thought people weren't getting married as much anymore either, but judging by the divorce settlements in my file cabinets I'm completely off.

Ah, yes, love in the time of pre-nuptial agreements and financial settlements. Very, very romantic.

I swear they must get married just to party for the night. Half the divorces we handle are couples who don't make it to the first five years.

Five years? Pretty much a lifetime these days.

Really Connie? Why bother?

Good question.

How long have your parents been married?

Fifty-one years.

Fifty-six for mine ... now that's a lifetime.

Can't compare our parent's time to these Rita. It's another world.

Why not? Love is still love.

Marriage meant something in those days; it was a different kind of contract back then.

I don't know about that.

Sure it was ... economics, religion, culture, all of that had a part. I don't really know what the attraction is today.

Same stuff seems to me. The allure of those stuffed envelopes of cash money, the partying, and the indulgence. Nothing like the cart and the mule our parents received when they got married.

Don't even mention the five-course meal and the stuffed pig and the sweet table and all that booze guzzled down, we really are a bunch of entitled gluttons.

I think we've moved on from the prosciutto and polenta under the grapevine ... and the accordion playing a tarantella ... ha, ha ... the good old days.

Are they still doing that?

Doing what? The cart and mule or the tarantella?

Shut up. I mean the really big wedding thing? The envelopes? The over the top stuff.

What? Where have you been living? When was the last time you went to a wedding reception? Haven't you noticed the invasion of banquet halls in this wasteland we live in? One bigger and more pretentious than the other on every acre of land that used to be a farm once.

You're way behind, my friend. They are called EVENT SPACES now. Get with the lingo.

Booked years in advance! Not just weddings but every other EVENT that we've decided needs celebration: endless boring showers and stags, fundraisers, the beatification of politicians and new saints, fools and "fashionistas" by the kilo. Are you kidding me? It's all about lifestyle.

I guess there's money to be made in weddings.

And funerals.

Spare me both.

Amen to that. Do you have any idea what weddings cost these days?

And funerals.

Death is a new industry.

I don't want a piece of that action.

They're charging over thirty grand for one of those mausoleum condos they've been building for "our eternal rest?" Death is a real business.

I'm sticking to travel, thank you very much.

Air conditioned, marble, wrought iron flower pots, they even pump music in when relatives visit. Well-ventilated, darling dead ones. You have to take out a mortgage now to be able to die. I think we've gone nuts.

Hey, do the *corna*! You don't want to bring bad luck talking about this stuff.

You still believe in the *corna*?

Doesn't hurt to be careful. Bad luck is bad luck. Come on, stick out your fingers, *corna*, *corna*, to bad luck.

It's not bad luck ... it's greed, pure and simple greed.

Okay, but it's bad luck too. So *corna* on you.

Greed and pretention ... look around, Connie, we're drowning in it.

Part of life, always has been.

Maybe.

What maybe? The world is what it is, my friend. It's all about money and progress. Don't tell me you've got something against progress?

Progress? Where's the responsibility? Progress without responsibility ... dangerous. Where are we going?

I think you might need a little more sugar, Rita. Can I get you another pastry?

Shut up. Does anyone have a little vision for the future? Maybe!

Why don't I order another little pastry for you. I'll get the one with the *ricotta* this time.

Go ahead make fun but we are out of control, especially in this community of ours. We can't just make a joke about it all the time with the "*fugget about it!*" Talk about stereotypes.

I get it, you've been surfing the documentary channel again and landed on David Suzuki, am I right? All that social conscience and farmed salmon and clean water. Not where we live.

You know what we've become, don't you? We're the "*tavola calda*" of the well-dressed and styled; no one takes us seriously. That's how they see us, you know, successful, arrogant, and tolerable. Jokes left and right about us ... but maybe they're right. What have we really done that's memorable?

Hey, come on now. We've done plenty of good things, don't be so negative.

Really?

Where would this country be without us? They'd still be drinking tea and eating cucumber sandwiches and putting ketchup on mushy pasta, come on Rita, ease up.

Yeah, yeah, I know, it's cool to drink cappuccino now.

Damn right it is. What's with you? We've given much more than cappuccino ... real sweat and real blood out there. My father cleared more wood in Sault St. Marie than Italy ever grew, and my mother washed and ironed for five boarders who worked on the railway lines, you should see the skin on her hands. Don't undervalue our achievements. Wasn't long ago my father and mother were made to feel like dirt in this country. Our fingerprint is on everything here, from concrete to cashmere. Shame on you, Rita. If I wanted tragedy on Friday, I'd watch one of those neo-realists you're always on about ... all that truth and humanity and art ... besides what's wrong with taking something back? We've earned it. Lighten up!

Sorry Connie, I didn't mean anything. I'm really tired and feeling my age ... damn menopause ... and full moon!

Great time to go into politics. We could use a menopausal woman to give them a run for their money. You said you always wanted to get into community affairs, go for it.

Once, maybe. Now it's too late. I haven't got the energy or the desire

It's never too late, to quote a cliché.

Holy shit, oh ... oh, my God, look! Look at who just walked in.

Who, where?

Jesus, Mary and Joseph, will you look at her ... look at that outfit! That must have cost a nickel or two for sure.

Who are you talking about?

There, the woman with the extensions, over there by the door. She just walked in. Boy you would never know it, not in a million years.

She's a tall one.

Not so tall without the shoes.

Those are really cool Jimmy Choo's. I've got a pair of those in red. So who is she? One of those new expatriate types?

Ex what?

Expatriate! The ones who arrive now and don't want to be known as immigrants. Italians off the Alitalia Airlines that's been bought by the Arabs.

Oh, no ... no, no ... she's one hundred percent immigrant, just like me.

And?

God just look at her, you would never be able to tell she used to crap in a pot once.

Crap where?

Look at her standing there all shiny and primped like a wedding *bomboniera*. Bet she doesn't remember that.

Do you know her?

I did once, a long time ago.

Where, when?

When we both flung crap over the balcony, in that nothing town we came from.

Holy crap? That sounds awful! Ha, ha ... excuse the pun ... ha, ha.

Yeah, it's funny now.

Come on, it is a little bit funny.

I remember giant rats at the bottom that would come and party in all the filth we let fly out of those windows and balconies.

Who is she?

Look ... at ... her ... now! How well she struts on those skinny heels.

Nice shoes though. You've got to admit.

That's her SUV out there with the SO SLEEK licence plate. I saw her getting out.

The Porche? Nice car. You've got to admit.

Sleek? How *cafone* can you get?

You going to tell me who she is or is this some kind of secret?

No secret. Just someone I used to know. Haven't seen her in years...

I emptied that pot over the balcony just like she did, but I haven't forgotten it.

Why don't you call her over?

I bet she washes her ass in a marble bidet now. Money can make you forget anything.

Maybe you should forget. It sounds disgusting.

Some things you can't forget.

Why would you want to remember something like that?

I don't know.

So why are you so bothered then? *"Fugget about it."* Easy enough.

Not so easy. It would cost me to forget.

Why should it cost you anything?

I don't know, I just know that it would.

How do you know it didn't cost her? Maybe she paid good money to some shrink to help her do it. Everybody is in therapy these days, maybe you should try it.

What would it cost *me* to forget?

I don't know what the Jesus you're asking. Do you mean the cost of a therapist? What do you mean?

That's because you've never had to shit in a pot and walk out to a balcony and throw it down below. Never had to clean it, or take in the putrid smell. To forget *that* would cost me something.

You're being a little dramatic don't you think? Rita, look around, we're in fucking Woodbridge. Get over it. It's done.

You're from Woodbridge, I just ended up here. It's where I am, but it isn't who I am.

Who you are? You are an office manager. You work for three rich lawyers who play golf on Friday. You live in a fifteen hundred square foot Condo and you eat pastries whenever you want. What are you whining about? Let it go, Rita, it's not that bad.

You don't know.

I was wrong about politics! Maybe you should take up acting.

It was no theatre. It was real.

Listen to you. Melodrama or what? So you were born in some shitty town like a million other assholes in this place, so what? You think a little crap over a balcony makes you a tortured soul? There are sadder stories than yours. Deal with it.

It's not so easy to forget some things. No matter how insignificant they seem.

Looks like it was easy for her.

Maybe I'd have to have her bank accounts to forget.

Maybe.

Or that *palazzo* with the pillars in the foyer and the five bathrooms where she can shit any time of day without ever seeing where it will land. That could make me forget ... maybe.

I think you're just a little jealous, my friend. That green-eyed monster is not a nice pet to have around.

Forgetting means she can sleep with that half man half goat she married because he could afford to buy her, and that makes it okay.

I think I smell a martyr burning...

Forgetting means she can spoil those arrogant baboons she gave birth to who spend her money faster than she can say *Dolce* and *Gabbana*.

You know an awful lot about her. Thought you hadn't seen her for ages.

Forgetting means she can walk right by us and we don't exist.

What? The woman hasn't even looked at us.

She can look down her nose at our Walmart exclusives and think *she's* better.

Walmart, my *cucuzze*... When have you ever bought anything at Walmart?

Toilet paper. I buy toilet paper at Walmart.

Wow ... you really don't like her do you? What's she ever done to you anyway? She looks harmless enough, except maybe for those nails. Wonder where she has them done?

I don't dislike her. Actually I loved her, once.

What did they slip into your cappuccino today? Maybe they spiked the pastry with something.

She was really sweet, once.

You're freaking me out a little. You going to tell me who she is, or do I call her over here myself?

We used to share a mattress a long time ago, slept head to foot. The pot was hidden under the bed. She's forgotten the first miserable years of our lives, removed herself from anyone who could remind her they ever existed.

Is she family?

Yes, she's family. She's history and memory? All the great big mortgages we never pay off. But I don't think it has cost her a single dime.

Look, she's waving at you. Go ahead, wave back. Go on, call her over.

Hello, Liliana? Is that you?

She's coming over.

Liliana! How are you? God it's been a long time.

More than a long time, Rita, much more. You look wonderful.

So do you, Liliana, I almost didn't recognize you, such a new look.

A girl needs some serious pruning once in a while.

How's the family? Your husband and kids?

They're good, Rita, thanks. Really, really good.

Your handsome husband still building those mansions up north?

Oh, yes, still in the business, subdivisions in Schomberg and Cookstown at the moment.

Moving on up as they say. And your kids?

Not kids anymore, Rita, they're all grown up. Matteo is in engineering, and Jessica is getting her degree in interior design. She's moved out. Bought a Condo downtown, in Liberty Village. Matteo is still at home for now. No reason to leave I guess; he has everything he needs at home. Boys seem to linger at home till they find a wife.

You must be proud of them.

Absolutely, they're terrific, and not just because they're mine.

What else would a proud mother say?

And you, what's happening with you Rita? What has life showered you with?

No husband, no children, no villa, just a cat and a litter box to empty. Nothing's changed.

Oh, I am sorry to hear that. I thought you might have married and had a family. You were always so good at taking care of people and things. You would have made a great mother.

Well not in this life; maybe in the next life I'll have a litter to spoil rotten.

Oh, no thank you very much, Rita, but this life is enough. Don't want to do it again in another one.

You're looking great Liliana, this life, marriage, suits you, obviously. Love the outfit, the shoes, and the extensions are wild.

Thanks, I try. Oh, but you are busy. Excuse me for interrupting.

No, no, excuse me. How rude. Meet my friend Costanzia Lamanna; I call her Connie

Nice to meet you, Costanzia, I'm Liliana Ranocchia.

Ranocchia? I've heard that name somewhere before.

It means frog in Italian, that's what you probably recognize.

What a great name! Tell me do you like green?

Ha, ha ... that's funny. Italians always have a good laugh at my name when they hear it. I always have to inform them, "by the way some frogs are brown."

Oh, yes, the toads. Well it could be worse, your name could be Porco! Ha, ha ... not that there is anything wrong with Porco, of course. As Shakespeare said, "what's in a name?"

When I first met my husband our friend Rita here used to joke that I had finally found my prince, "The Frog." Remember Rita?

Some things you cannot forget Liliana. We were just talking about that before you hopped in.

Rita has a sense of humour, but I am sure you know that already, Costanzia.

Anyway it is nice to meet you, Liliana. Love your Jimmy Choo's.

I know, Costanzia, aren't they amazing? I have a closet full. I love shoes, can't get enough of them.

Just like Imelda.

Imelda?

Oh, nobody important, just another lover of shoes like you and Connie. Why don't you join us, Liliana? We can catch up, talk about old times.

I'd love to, Rita, some other time, for sure, definitely some other time.

No better time than the present they say.

True, but I've got to run now. I have a Brazilian scheduled. Not looking forward to it but must be done.

I thought they had forbidden further waxing of the Brazilian rainforest ... ha, ha.

I can see why you two are friends, both funny ladies. I envy your sense of humour. I can never make jokes.

Oh, don't do that, Liliana. Don't envy us. There is nothing to envy. We're just a couple of *zitelle* on the hunt for the meaning of life. And I may have found mine in shoes ... ha, ha.

Well, it was great to meet you, Costanzia, and really great to see you again, Rita. You really haven't changed much at all, not at all.

You have. Oh, I mean, you look terrific, really, really ... sleek.

I try.

Ciao, ciao, Liliana ... great to see you.

You too.

Oh, careful there, Lily, watch the steps, those shoes can do some serious damage if you fall off.

It took a while but I have mastered the art of walking in them. I'm a pro.

I can see that.

Nice meeting you, Costanzia.

See you at the shoe store, Liliana.

Great bumping into you again, Liliana. Remember those days we ran around without shoes?

I try not to Rita. It's easier that way.

I suppose it is. Hope to see you again soon, *cugina.*

I won't forget, Rita. Promise.

Oh, but you will.

Ciao, ciao.

A GIRL MADE OF LAVENDER

...[T]o store
the memories of love.
Little adulteress,
before they punished you.
—Seamus Heaney, "Punishment"

I CAN STILL SMELL LYNNE'S WHITE starched blouse with the delicate lace collar that buttoned at the back of her neck. The faint scent floated around her perfect head. Her pristine cotton skirt with the yellow buttons down the side was perfectly ironed and crisp and resting above her pink knees. The subtle fragrance of her radiant, translucent skin had welcomed me into the classroom as I sat in the seat next to her at Gledhill Public that first school day in September.

Lynne was the first Canadian girl I saw when I walked into Mrs. Riley's third grade class the year I came to Canada. The first girl who smelled like something I had never smelled before. She was thin and white and straight and she sat in her seat like a girl in a painting. Lynne was brand new. Lynne looked like Canada. Lynne smelled like Canada. My black uncombed curls and the homemade dress that hung on my lumpy frame made me a little ashamed. I was unscented. I was dark and spotted with moles and without starch or lace.

From that first day when I sat beside her, I wanted to be Lynne. I wanted to look like Lynne and to smell like Lynne. I wanted my homemade dress to be starched and clean like her blouse and I wanted a lace collar around my neck. I later learned that her perfect, clean, starched blouse was sprayed with lavender. She was forever stuck inside my nose, a girl made of lavender.

Darrel and Billy who sat behind us in class were both in love with Lynne and she knew it. She knew it every time she took the Jersey milk chocolate bars they stole for her from Henry's Five and Ten Cent store down the street. Every day it was a contest between the two boys. Who could earn her love with the sweetest candies or the best chocolate stolen from Henry's Five and Ten Cent store?

Billy got caught once filling both pockets of his pants with goodies and Henry, the store owner, dragged him to the principal's office. Billy's mother had to come to the school. She was really mad and you could hear her screaming at Billy all the way down the hallway. She was really loud. But it didn't stop Billy; he was too much in love. Billy simply switched stores and the very next day, after his mother had done all that screaming, Billy brought Lynne goodies he'd picked up on his way to school at the Woolworth's on the corner of Woodbine and Danforth.

Darrel was Billy's best friend even though they were always trying to outdo each other to win Lynne's affection. Darrel was a quiet sort, and he followed Lynne everywhere she went. Every recess and every lunch hour after school he'd wait by the fence till she appeared. His eyes were always crammed with her white beauty, her immaculate clothes, and her sweet smell.

Darrel loved bringing her presents, particularly little figurines of animals, some made of glass, some made of wood. He would wrap them in pink Kleenex and whenever Lynne appeared he would hand them to her with a smile that showed all his crooked teeth. I wondered where he got all the little animal figurines, because they looked as if they cost a lot of money, but he never told anyone where they came from. They just seemed to appear every week, like magic, a new little animal would pop out of his pocket wrapped in pink Kleenex. Darrel loved animals. He mostly loved horses and would draw them on big sheets of coloured paper. The drawings were beautiful and they looked almost real, like photographs taken with a camera. He drew the horses for Lynne but she preferred the little glass animals. She always threw the drawings away. I found one she had thrown away in the schoolyard one day. A white horse with wings and Lynne's name printed in blue letters on the back. I knew it was one that Darrel had drawn. I took it home and hung it in our basement kitchen.

Darrel and Billy lived for Lynne. The other boys made fun of them, but Darrel and Billy didn't care. They guarded Lynne like a princess. They protected her from anything that didn't shine like she did, and always made sure she had plenty of sweets, little animal figurines and drawings of beautiful horses, to keep her company.

Lynne hardly ever played with the girls. She didn't skip double-dutch or jump over the elastic band ropes we made. She didn't soil her clothes with dodge ball or baseball like the rest of us. Lynne never once played with me. Every recess she was busy with her boys, unwrapping something special.

Lynne had tiny perfect ears, like those tiny shells from the sea. I could see them because her hair was always in a ponytail, tied with a shiny blue ribbon and her perfect ears were always there, in my eyes. The elastic that held my unruly curls together was thick and brown, and my ears were not pretty.

Lynne's head was also just the right size. I would stare at it sometimes and watch her ponytail swish back and forth as she moved. I watched her, hoping that once, just once, she would turn and see me. She never did.

Mrs. Riley wasn't sure what to do with me that first day I walked into her class, all frizzy-curled and awkward. She sat me next to Lynne hoping her light would somehow creep into me. It never did. Even when I tried to copy everything Lynne would do. I sat the way she sat, back straight at her desk. I held my head up the way she did on her long skinny neck. I stared at the blackboard the way she did, even when there was nothing on the board to look at. I watched how her fingers moved her pencil, how she printed her letters and her numbers so neatly between the lines on the workbook page. I tried to do the same but I never understood why the numbers and letters had to stay so neatly between the lines. I never asked, but I did it anyway.

The day Cristina came into our room, Mrs. Riley moved me to the back of the class next to Brenda who didn't have a smell at all but was very tall. Cristina was new to Gledhill Public just like me. She came from an island in the middle of the ocean. Mrs. Riley said that Cristina came from a place called Greece and that she didn't speak any English at all. The teacher didn't know what to do with her either but she must have thought Cristina needed Lynne more than I did because she gave her my desk next to Lynne. I didn't want to move. I liked sitting next to Lynne even if she never looked at me or talked to me. Sitting next to Lynne made me think that one day I could smell like lavender and someone would steal Jersey milk chocolate bars just for me. I wanted to sit next to Lynne forever, but now Cristina needed Lynne more than I did. Cristina's sad crossed eyes told me that.

I moved next to Brenda who had no smell at all. Her tall head hid Lynne's pretty ears so I could not see them from where I was sitting. Brenda's hair didn't move like Lynne's ponytail. It just sat flat and brown, without ribbons, on her shoulders. Brenda chewed her fingernails one by one, spitting the bits on the pages of my book, *Run Spot, Run,* that Mrs. Riley had given me to help me learn to read in English. I missed Lynne's see-through skin and her wonderful smell.

*

It was a long walk down Danforth Avenue to Woodbine from Gledhill Public. Nobody lived as far from the school as I did, except for Cristina who lived on Aldergrove Avenue, the dead end street near the railway track. I lived on Moberly, the street that led to the railway track. Lynne didn't have to walk much at all. She lived a few houses from the school and she went home for lunch every day. Her mother always waited for her on the veranda with a pretty flowered apron tied around her waist and a pink-lipped smile. Cristina and I ate our big messy sandwiches in the schoolyard and when we were finished we played with our skipping ropes without talking. We skipped and waited for the others to return from lunch and for the bell to ring.

Sometimes Cristina followed me home after school, but always a few steps behind me. If I stopped, she stopped. If I moved, she moved. One day I turned around and looked at her and she caught up to me. We tried to talk to each other, but she didn't understand me much and I didn't understand her. We walked together anyway. She had these odd crossed eyes that stared at her own nose and they seemed a bit funny so that I wanted to giggle a little, but I never did.

The day Mrs. Riley left to have her baby, Lynne cried. Lynne was Mrs. Riley's favourite, the student with all the gold stars next to her name on the bulletin board of excellence. But that day, when Mrs. Riley left, Lynne looked different. I watched tears slide down her perfect face leaving little wet spots on her clean starched blouse. I felt sad for Lynne. I was sure that girls made of lavender with seashell ears and swishy ponytails, who ate Jersey milk chocolate bars, and were loved by boys would never, ever have to cry.

The new teacher wasn't nice like Mrs. Riley. She had a wrinkled face full of brown spots. Her lips were cracked at the side where her spit gathered when she talked and she never smiled. She walked up and down between the rows of seats, back and forth, staring at our faces and slapping her hands together. The new teacher sat Cristina next to me in the last seat by the window in the fifth row. Now I couldn't see Lynne at all from where I was sitting. I couldn't smell her or watch her ponytail bounce back and forth. Lynne's perfect head and sea-shell ears had disappeared. Now, all I had was Cristina's ears, big and round, with small gold loops in each one. Cristina didn't chew her fingernails. She didn't smell like lavender, more like lemon. She didn't look like Canada and her hair was sort of wild without ribbons or elastics. We sat together in the last two seats of the fifth row where nobody ever passed by, but from that day on we walked home together after school every day. Sometimes we'd read from *Run, Spot, Run* and soon we learned to speak to each other in words we both understood.

On our way to and home from school, we would pass the Woolworths store. Sometimes we'd press our noses to the window and look at all the nice things inside, but we never had any money to spend, or a Billy or Darrel who would steal for us. One day we decided we would begin to save our coppers and when we had saved enough we would go into Woolworths and buy a miniature bottle of lavender water and a Jersey milk chocolate bar. Weeks and weeks went by until we had finally saved enough money. We excitedly walked into Woolworths and headed towards the make-up counter and picked up a tiny bottle of lavender water. We carefully counted the exact amount and paid with all of our saved coppers. We rushed outside and sprayed it all over our clothes and all over our hair and skin. But neither one of us smelled like Lynne at all. We wrapped the little bottle that was still half full in a pink Kleenex and left it on Lynne's desk the next day in school. Cristina and I knew that lavender belonged to Lynne and it would never smell the same on girls like us.

MY MOTHER, MY FATHER, MY SINS

...[T]his river in which the past
is always flowing, every water
is the same water coming round.
—Lucille Clifton, "The Mississippi River Empties into the Gulf"

BY THE TIME CARLO WAS BORN, I had survived eleven years of my mother and my father. The one great triumph Carlo claimed over me was being born a boy. But when he arrived, all eight pounds of him, round and sausage soft, with wispy molasses curls, he wasn't welcomed with any notable ceremony by either of my parents, regardless of his favoured gender. All the expectations that come from being a male child should have set bells ringing, like a cathedral at Christmas. He should have been celebrated with fireworks like New Years Eve. But my house was quiet. There was no merriment. There were no voices bellowing the glorious arrival of the carrier of our history. There were no candy-covered almonds to sweeten the mouths of relatives and friends who had ventured to our house bringing good wishes and soup. Carlo was the child born in a bed at Doctor's Hospital on Brunswick

Avenue, attended by Canadian nurses and wrapped in warm blue blankets. His entry into our world was slow and painful for my mother. For forty-two hours she held in the screams and waited, unlike my quick exit on the kitchen floor of a hut in the little village she had left behind. A village built around a stone quarry where my father had apprenticed as a stone mason when he was a young man. In Canada my father did not work with stone, did not carve anything in marble, but dug deep holes underground where miles and miles of pipes curve underneath an immense, cold city.

When Carlo was brought home one week after his birth, my mother handed him to me, walked into her bedroom, and closed the door.

Eleven years before Carlo was born, my parents had landed in the port of Halifax, with two suitcases and me. It was the year President John Fitzgerald Kennedy was assassinated. This was always a point of reference whenever my parents spoke of their arrival, because they had both been charmed by the great and handsome American president. My father, in conversation with acquaintances, would often refer to that year as the "*anno tragico.*" I had always assumed the tragedy he referred to was the death of his beloved President Kennedy, but in years to come I understood that assumption may have been wrong.

The distance that existed between my father and me had been there from the time I could remember. My earliest memory might be at age four. I can still see a man who never smiled, a man whose laughter I never heard. I missed the laughter I heard in other men when I watched them play with their children on the street and on the verandas of our neighbourhood. I wondered why my father never held my hand and never walked me to the nearby park. My presence seemed to make him uncomfortable. He was not cruel or angry or in any way unkind, he simply wasn't interested. When he did speak to me for any reason, it was with a dismissive tone, as if nothing I had to say would be of any concern or importance. I know now that he must have mourned the incapability of my female birth to have procured his immortality, and therefore he had little to do with me for those eleven years before my brother entered the world. It would become Carlo's task to make my father immortal. But by then it was too late even for Carlo. Too many years had passed between the need and the dream, and in his late forties my father was already tired and lost. I know now that he had abandoned the thought of immortality both in name and spirit and instead retreated into his sanctuary of wine and cheeses where he could indulge his pleasures alone, without interruption.

Carlo's advent all those years after my arrival could not resurrect my father from his constructed catacomb, where he spent most of his free hours locking the cellar door behind him. The contentment he found among the bottles and the fermented milks he prepared for himself was beyond anything my mother, Carlo, or I could offer him. He no longer cared for eternal life or reality; he had found the darkness that suited him best.

*

My mother, who should have rejoiced in the light of her second child, began to manifest the strangest behaviour towards the newborn, preferring always to hand him over to others, as if holding him was an assignment she did not enjoy. Allowing his cries to become unbearable and leaving him alone in his crib. When I would return from school she would quickly hand him to me as if she were unloading a burdensome sack. Then, she would retreat to her bedroom and close the door. I am convinced now that my mother and father had never wanted children at all. Carlo and I were an unfortunate accident of time, place, and necessity. Our father ignored us. And as for my mother, there was no warmth in her embraces, no light in her eyes when she looked at either Carlo or me. I might have hated her all of those years, but I was not able to. I am sure I loved her, whatever love was between us.

I don't recall much of the very early years, before coming to Canada. They might have been fine or not. Some moments come in bits and pieces when I try to remember. It shouldn't really matter, those years are done and gone, except now I have chosen to re-visit everything in conversation with the objective ear of a therapist. Sitting in an office with beige walls and prints of wildflowers on the twenty-seventh floor of a downtown building, I am looking for my mother and my father.

What comes back over and over is my mother's silence. She stopped talking and only looked at me with tired eyes, drained eyes. Only the sudden flick of her hands and fingers communicated her needs. This happened about the same time my father had found refuge in his cavern. His presence had become a shadow that moved in the hallway of our house and then fled down the basement stairs. My mother's silence followed.

My mother's activities were generally confined to the kitchen and when the chores were done and the house was clean, she would sit and crochet endless tablecloths that were never used, but were always folded neatly and placed in a chest that stood beneath the mirror of her bedroom wall. Her fingers moved with the same silence that lived around her. While she crocheted and my father hid in the cellar, I took care of Carlo. The one blessing, he was a pleasant child.

The continuing lunacy that is my mother's silence seems almost clearer to me now that she no longer makes sense of anything at all. For many years growing up I blamed myself for my mother's unhappiness, her silence, believing I was the reason she would not speak. I had wanted her attention, her embrace, but it never came. Only once do I clearly remember her arms around me, the day I received my first communion. A brief moment that I hoped would be repeated. It was not. I attributed her distance to something in me that was defective, inadequate. But I was wrong. There was nothing defective about me, my therapist assures me.

The solitary refugee that was my father I think I now also understand. Since his death years ago, I have made peace and there is no more anger. It has become a game of sort to understand the reasons of his indifference. My father had refused life as it had been dealt to him. He particularly could not handle the life he had to re-interpret, or reinvent, when he arrived in a new country. It had never been his choice to leave his Italy. It had been decided for him by his elders, as most things in his life had been decided. My mother was not the woman he would have chosen to marry, but simply the woman he had been expected to marry, to complete the idea of place and family. That they were first cousins and had been promised in marriage by brothers intent on keeping their properties in the family was not unusual in those backward towns. That there was no love or even attraction between them is also not unusual. In those days, in those towns, this must have been common in many marriages. Their sadness turned tragic when it was packed into two suitcases and sent away over the ocean with me by their side. That was the year they landed on Beatrice Avenue in the month of November.

My father had always indulged in anything that could temporarily disconnect him from his reality. His long hours of work in the deep holes of construction were not kind. He was not suited for the physical labour he endured all those years. The responsibility of family, especially one he had not wanted, was overwhelming for him, but he endured. My mother had no voice with which to explain her unhappiness. Her ties to me as a small child kept her prisoner on Beatrice Avenue. The language she spoke rarely, she did not teach me, as if it was something she wanted to keep only for herself, and the one I learned to speak she wanted no part of. I understood her signals. It was a language we developed for each other without words. Whatever misfortune was my parent's marriage it should not have been my responsibility, but it was, and I lived in its gloom until my father's death the year I turned twenty-nine. My father's death was for my mother a relief and perhaps her liberation.

It wasn't Carlo's fault being born a boy much too late in their lives to have resuscitated hope. It was not his fault he could not possibly repair what was broken between them, and it wasn't my fault that I was born a girl. Both of us were wrong for our family, it seemed. We were simply the reason or the consequence that knotted four twisted people together. My brother Carlo left Beatrice Avenue when he was barely seventeen. One day he packed a gym bag, left a note on the kitchen table, and walked out the front door. He did not return until my father's death, and then only for a very short while.

If I ask myself how long my mother will go on in her silence,

I can either erupt into laughter or tears; they are equal. My mother continues to exist in her silence even now that she is beyond old and I am still the presence she endures. We are now two old women who share a house in a city she has never really known. A city that has played host to five decades of her life, all of them lived on the same street where she has wandered away only on occasion. She still has the use of her legs without the need of a cane, but she can only manage to the bottom of the street, then she tires and stands and waits. It puzzles me how she occasionally manages to open the safety locks I have put in place, to keep her inside while I allow myself a ten-minute shower. I cherish that moment of peace in my day, but somehow it doesn't matter how well I secure our fortress on Beatrice Avenue, she finds a way to get out. Sometimes a generous neighbour leads her back to our door when I am late in noticing her exit.

I retired from my position at the Bank of Montreal earlier than I had wanted to because I could not live with the guilt of placing my mother in a nursing home. I have a new occupation: caregiver. And like any good daughter, I take the role seriously. My brother Carlo has decided he wants nothing to do with either of us, having chosen a lifestyle that has no room for what he calls "desperate" women. He asked, politely and clearly, to be left alone. I have acknowledged his request.

Carlo's disconnection from my mother is not a surprise. There had been little contact between them while he was growing up. If I am honest, he was ashamed of what he referred to as "her small immigrant life" and her silence. His rejection of me is a little more puzzling. It surprises me that he no longer recalls I was also his caregiver once. Those years when my mother retreated from him and locked herself into her dimness, I became the mother. I became the substitute. It might have been an undiagnosed depression that cast the shadows over my mother after Carlo was born, a complete retreat from her newborn child. She was unwilling to hold him or feed him or love him. She forfeited that responsibility to me. Carlo has conveniently forgotten the role I played in his young life.

I remember an incident when his cries were so violent there was no way to pacify him and no matter what I tried, from lullabies to bottles, nothing seemed to help. His little body in continuous spasm, I was afraid he would drop from my hands. My mother took pity on me when Carlo's cries became unbearable and she could see the fear in my eyes.

"*Dammelo,*" she demanded.

My mother held out her arms and I passed the screaming baby over to her. She took him, sat in a chair, placed him on her lap and began to unbundle him. I watched her expose his squirming body to the air. With the palm of her hand she rubbed circles around his heaving tummy, round and round. Then she slowly bent her head over him, and her lips opened and took in Carlo's tiny penis. She began sucking lightly and gently on it while her hand continued to rest on his tummy. The baby's cries lessened and gradually he calmed. When she lifted her head the look on her face was expressionless. She wrapped him in the blanket and quietly said, "*prendilo.*"

I took Carlo and cradled him gently as she walked away, closing her bedroom door firmly behind her.

I had never seen her so tender toward either one of us before. It was a gentle act she performed on Carlo, with none of the violence she had offered me while I was growing into a young woman. But I have forgiven all those daily inspections she violated on me when I would return from school during my teenage years. Her rough hands between my legs, lifting my skirts, pulling down my panties, checking to see if I had been bad, if there were signs of my wicked ways. She never asked me if I had been with a boy, never offered any words to explain my becoming a woman. Only her looks spoke in the unforgiving way eyes speak when they are filled with disappointment. If I had been the reason for her disappointment it would have made sense, but it was not me she was punishing, my therapist assures me.

I remained a virgin longer than she would ever have believed. The barbarity of her inspections, the constant terror at the possible loss of my virginity, became an obsession. She harboured many fears inside that gloom she brought with her from another place. But it was never men that would be my downfall. That is the irony. The promiscuity I indulged in years later, when she could no longer assault what was between my legs with her accusing fingers, was not about men. It was about revenge. There were nights when I purposely would not return home, wanting her to worry, wanting her to suffer, imagining what I was up to. There were periods when I thought I might leave, escape, but I never did. I still don't understand the bond, the concealed shackles that keep us tied to our tormenters forever. I was a woman who could have run away but I didn't and I cannot tell you why.

I sought out men who had wives, who had other commitments, and would not demand any loyalty. There were boyfriends who wanted to be loved and I would refuse, needing only their attention and not their affection. I am a spinster by choice and not by Carlo's definition of desperate and old.

My mother's complete decline into dementia is now the final act of this theatre of the bizarre that has been our life together.

I should grieve the disappearance of my mother as others claim they grieve when faced with this disease. I have friends whose pain at the loss of a parent's memory is more legitimate than mine. I am reluctant to allow myself any more grief; it has already been recorded. I now perform the duties expected of me. I bathe my mother's body to remove the odour that comes with incontinence. I wipe away all that escapes from her body, without control, and feel no indignity. I feed her. I place her in the chair by the window where the sun comes into the room. I indulge her with her favourite sweets. I organize the pills and the creams. I read her passages from her book of saints even if the language it is written in is foreign to me. I continue speaking to her in my language when I attempt to communicate at all. Whether after all these years she has understood any of my words is still a mystery.

The strangest mystery of all is that my mother recognizes my face but not her own. I have had to cover all the mirrors in the house. Her own face frightens her, as if there is an intruder in her presence and she attacks her reflection with fists in an act of self-defense. The violence of the attacks on her reflected image has resulted in some severe cuts to her arms and knuckles. Yet her hands and fingers have not forgotten how to perform in a quiet and creative manner. She can sit for hours crocheting, gently pulling that needle in and out of those tiny loops, composed and peaceful. The speed with which her fingers move is fascinating to watch. I find myself unravelling the tablecloths to re-cycle the threads and keep her occupied. I feel a small stitch of guilt at my indifference to the work she produces, but the cost of keeping her in threads and wools would not be practical. Besides, there are too many tablecloths stuffed into drawers that no one will use, too many blankets that gather more dust than memory. This my therapist will analyze without doubt.

Twelve hours a week I have a respite. A woman named Soleya provides me with short-term relief. Four hours every other day except weekends, I can disappear and leave my mother's silence to a stranger. My mother is free of me for twelve hours each week.

During my hours of freedom, I walk to the Sicilian Café at the corner of Montrose and College, a block away from our house on Beatrice. The habit is routine. I pick up a newspaper from the local variety store, stop to look at the fruits and vegetables at Kenny's market, decide on what to buy on my way home. On occasion I also look in at the used book store, generally thumbing through their dollar bin for some literary jewel I might find. There are few jewels in a dollar bin but once I found a book with an intriguing title, *The Sky With Its Mouth Wide Open,* for seventy-five cents. One of the best books I have ever read. So I keep looking in the dollar bin.

The large windows at the Sicilian Café are perfect for spying on the world as it passes by. I sit at a table facing south, watching the streetcars crawl to a stop as they approach the traffic light, and the incessant parade of bicycles swerving in and out of traffic as car horns argue their intrusive space. I order a coffee from the young waiter with the snake tattoo that circles his neck. I stare at his earlobes. There are two quarter-sized holes in each. Another mystery I will not decipher. The few remaining old women in the neighbourhood are bent over their four-wheeled carriages that steady them as they head toward the Metro Supermarket. Any one of them could be my mother. They are me, not so far into my future. I wonder about their stories, curious about their lives. I wonder if their recollections are filled with more joy than regrets. So many shopping carts to lean on, carts that keep us from falling.

The coffee arrives with the bubbling chocolate foam sliding down the side of the cup. I spoon the creamy thickness to my lips as I flip through the pages of the newspaper. I am intrigued by an article in the Life Section on the subject of women. I read the first sentence: "The lives of immigrant women are not interesting enough to be put on the stage."

I knock over my cup, spill my coffee. The words on the page swell and merge into a blend of sweet chocolate and ink. I cannot stop laughing. My therapist will love this.

ACKNOWLEDGEMENTS

To my husband Andrew, and my daughter Gia, who insist on loving me even when the full moon has settled in for long visits. Nothing much would matter without you.

To my mother, Antonietta, who at ninety-one is beautiful and filled with songs, and whose love of people and life is infectious; I hope you are contagious and I've inherited your genes.

To my friends (too many to name), forever faithful and supportive, and to those friends who have gone and continue in another dimension, you are loved.

To my sister, nieces, and nephews, and my extended family in Italy, New Zealand, Australia, and Canada, I wish you all lived next door. Miss you always.

To my publisher at Inanna, and my editor, Luciana Ricciutelli, for taking a chance; I'm honoured.

To my friend, artist, Mimmo Baronello for his brilliant painting on the cover of my book, I am so grateful.

To my first publishers Guernica Editions, LyricalMyrical Press, and Quattro Books for accepting my first words.

To Theresa Carilli and Oriana Palusci, for your advice, friendship and continued support, you are sisters in the soul.

To the women and men who inspired my stories, thank you, thank you.

A previous version of "Painted Windows" was published in *Daughters for Sale* (1997).

A previous version (poem) of "A Girl Made of Lavender" was published in *Too Much Love (*2012).

"My Grandmother is Normal" was first published in *Canadian Woman Studies/les cahiers de la femme* (2013).

Credits:

Maria Terrone. "The Tatted Handkerchief." *Embroidered Stories: Interpreting Women's Domestic Needlework from the Italian Diaspora*. Eds. Edvige Giunta and Joseph Sciorra. Jackson, MS: University Press of Mississippi, 2014.

Patrizia Cavalli. "Ma questo non é sonno." *Poesie: 1974-1992.* Turin: G. Einaudi, 1992.

Pier Paolo Pasolini, qtd. in Luciana Bohne. "Becoming Neorealism." *Counterpunch*, November 6, 2015.

Eavan Boland. "Love." *In a Time of Violence: Poems*. New York: W. W. Norton & Co, 1995. First published in 1994.

Mary Di Michele."Mimosa." *Mimosa and Other Poems*. Oakville, ON: Mosaic Press, 1981.

Dylan Thomas. "Do Not Go Gentle into That Good Night." *The Poems of Dylan Thomas*. New Revised Edition. New York: New Directions Publishing, 2003.

James K. Baxter. "Moss on Plum Branches." *Collected Poems of James K. Baxter*. Ed. John Edward Weir. Oxford, UK: Oxford University Press, 2004.

Dionne Brand. "ossuary 1." *Ossuaries*. Toronto: Penguin Random House Canada, 2010.

Gia Milne-Allan (my daughter): She knows me better than I know myself and reminds me of it, constantly.

Eavan Boland. "What We Lost." *Outside History: Selected Poems, 1980-1990*. New York: W.W. Norton & Co., 1991.

Lawrence Ferlinghetti. "Challenges to Young Poets." *San Francisco Poems: Lawrence Ferlinghetti*, Poet Laureate Series Number 1. San Francisco: City Lights Foundation, 1991.

Rose Romano. "This is Real." *The Wop Factor*. Brooklyn/ Palermo: Malafemmina Press, 1994.

T. S. Eliot. "The Love Song of J. Alfred Prufrock." *T. S. Eliot. The Complete Poems and Plays of T. S. Eliot.* Boston: Faber, 1969.

Seamus Heaney. "Punishment." *North.* London: Faber & Faber, 1975.

Lucille Clifton. "The Mississippi River Empties into the Gulf." *The Collected Poems of Lucille Clifton 1965-2010.* American Poets Continuum. Ed. Kevin Young and Michael S. Glaser Foreword by Toni Morrison. Rochester, NY: BOA Editions, 2012.

Photo: Andrew Milne-Allan

Gianna Patriarca was born in Italy and immigrated in 1960 as a child. Her publications include seven books of poetry and one children's book. Her first collection, *Italian Women and Other Tragedies*, was runner-up to the Milton Acorn People's Poetry Award and in 2009 was translated into Italian and launched at the university of Bologna and Naples. *My Etruscan Face* was shortlisted for the Bressani Literary Award in 2009. Her work is extensively anthologized in many Canadian, American, and Italian publications, and is on university course lists in all three countries. Her work has also been adapted for the stage and for CBC radio drama, and has been part of the documentary Pier 21 with TLN. She lives and works in Toronto.